The
Last
Catamount

Copyright 2025

…because we need to realize that other animals are evolving along this same developmental model, and in a direction very similar to our own. So it's not at all ludicrous to ask ourselves if some of the more advanced species may have already begun going through the experience of becoming self-aware. I mean, there's a good chance it's started to happen in the animal kingdom.

Holy shit. What would it be like to be a whale, or an elephant, or an octopus, and have to go through that totally crushing experience of becoming aware of yourself? I'm not talking about the mere knowledge that you exist; that happens when we're toddlers and it's no big deal anyway. I'm talking about the realization that the days of just you and the rest of the world are over. In marches some uninvited third wheel who takes it upon itself to watch (and *judge*, though it'll never admit it) virtually everything you do. And it never so much as steps out for a coffee break. *It's there all the time.* That's the real kicker. I'm pretty sure I could tolerate occasional small rations of self-awareness. Maybe a few minutes every week or so would suffice; you know, to assess what kind of progress I've been making with my life and all that stuff. I might actually be OK with that kind of an arrangement.

But NO. The day it arrived, it decided to move in permanently. You could never escape it, especially when you really *needed* to escape it. Because *it* was *me*. How the fuck did that happen?

I don't know how, but I can tell you when, at least in my own case. I'd just started high school and I was walking home one day, turning the corner from Ljepava Drive to Shadow Mountain Drive in the eerily empty streets of upper middle-class Suburbia, California, when it struck from above, diving stealthily out of an endlessly blue sky and hitting me right over the head.

The rest of the way home, all I could think about were those not so distant times of pretending to shoot each other as we ran across the front lawns of summer evenings when all the kids were allowed outside, even after dinner, and the goal was to make the most spectacular high-speed wipe-out death roll possible after getting shot. I kept thinking how I could never again do that kind of thing without watching from some far-off spot, analyzing and assessing every movement, churning it through the kind of mind shit that takes away all the fun.

Can you imagine having to go through that as an elephant? Or an octopus? It would be trippy, but it would also be very, very heavy.

-Attributed to Jacques Cousteau

If we are to walk any further together, we need to have this agreement: You will not think me a bullshitter and I will not bullshit. I have neither the need nor the ability to do so. Despite what you'll read about in later chapters, and despite how I may challenge your understanding of the true nature of catamounts, you have to take my word for it. Because if we can't agree on that, then you should walk away right now, and I should turn and make two giant leaps for the safety of the forest…

Chapter 1

"Jesus H. Christ! Can't we at least agree no earlier than…"

"Rodney?"

"What the fuck is it, James? Can't you see I'm actually trying to compromise here? Can't you see I've given up?"

"I'm sorry to have to interrupt you like this, Rodney, but I believe his proper middle name is *Fuckin'*, so that would make it *Jesus F. Christ*. That's all. Sorry, just a technicality. Please continue."

"You are one fucking work of art, James. One real fucking work of art. Anyway, I think you can see I've given up any hope of saving it for the last chapter, even though that is undoubtedly our best play. But, if it has to be early, can't we at least agree to hold off until the second chapter? I mean, really!"

Now the author spoke. "You think it needs to be at the end as some kind of hook, that the only thing that'll keep them reading is the anticipation of some BIG REVEAL at the end? That's ridiculous. They don't even know it's there. It's not part of the plot, you know. It's not like finding out the identity of the murderer or who dies at the end."

"Yeah, I know. But people read first chapters in bookstores, for chrissakes, and I think we do actually want to sell a few books. I mean, the last time I looked, that was kind of important. Maybe not so much nowadays."

"Of course it's important, Rodney. We're with you there. Absolutely, right with you. It's just that this isn't the reason they're buying. It's kind of like an unexpected surprise."

"Bonus material!"

"Yes. Not the plot or the characters or any of that other stuff they want. Oh, don't worry, we'll do just fine in those areas as well. But since this…." The author turned to James. "What would you call it, anyway?"

"Revelation?"

"Unveiling?"

"Mind-Blowing Shit?"

"OK, whatever you call it, it's just extra, that's all. They'll have no idea it's even there, so if you're thinking it's going to keep them turning the pages, well, that's ridiculous."

Now the author spoke again. "Listen, they're either fans or they aren't fans. If they're fans, they'll read every page regardless. If not, then they're probably not going to buy the book in the first place. So why not tell them right up front? Very first chapter. Get it out of the way."

There was a bit of silence before Rodney ran with the bait. "Fans? Are you serious? You think there are millions of fans out there just hovering over your every word? In case you haven't noticed, the last time we counted you've got a total of eight fans: your wife, that lady in the house down the hill, your college friend in Oregon, that cousin in LA, and just to be generous we'll give you his sister as well, although we're not really sure about her. What does that make?"

"Five."

"OK. Then there are six unknowns out there who have read only one of your books, so we cut that in half to give you three more, and you end up with eight. Fans, that is."

"Jonathan?" James turned to the author and tried to get his attention. "Jonathan?"

"Yes, what is it?"

"Your father died."

"Thank you, James, for reminding me of that."

"No, what I mean is, that cuts out twelve percent of your former base."

"Yes," added Rodney, "and that segment had the highest enthusiasm ratings across the board. It's not a good development."

Now a longer silence settled over the table before Rodney summarized. "I'm not trying to make light of your fan statistics. I wouldn't be here if I didn't believe in you, so who knows, maybe I'm a fan too. But even if we included all of us, your fan base might not be the best starting point for making decisions on how best to move forward. What do you think?"

The author remained calm. "All I said is that a fan is a fan from the very first word. And if so, every sentence will be read. There's no need for baiting strategies to keep my readers involved."

James had been silent through this exchange, but now he spoke up. "How can someone be a fan from the very first word? That doesn't make any kind of sense."

"Because he or she has always been a fan."

Now Rodney scoffed. "Oh, it's more of your metaphysical mumbo jumbo, is it?" He looked at the author but all he got was a shrug of the shoulders, so he continued in a voice not even trying to hide his annoyance. "And you've already admitted that this bit has nothing whatsoever to do with the storyline, the characters, or anything else in the book, right?"

"For the most part, yes."

"Then why the fucking hell are we even including it in the first place?"

"Because I think the readers will like it." He paused, then added, "It's only a few fairly short paragraphs."

Before Rodney could lash into him once again, James unexpectedly came to his defense. "Yes, yes, I agree, absolutely. To sit on this would be…negligence, betrayal even."

Rodney remained unconvinced but realized he wasn't about to get his way on this one. "Fine. I don't care. We'll find ourselves buried deep in the *Spirituality* stack. You know, that's the one on the second floor way in the back next to the bathrooms, which, by the way, is as far from that shelf as most of those books ever get. So can we just get on with it, then?"

"Yeah, I think it's time," said the author.

"So the first chapter will begin with the *calling* thing, and we'll save your mumbo jumbo for at least chapter two."

"Maybe…"

"What do you mean, *maybe*?"

"You're just going to have to wait and see, just like all the rest of them."

"Fuckin'-A." Rodney stood and glared at the other two. "All right, fine. Have it your way. But there is something seriously wrong here. As an example: this whole beginning. What the fuck kind of start to a novel is this? I mean, I don't even know myself who we're supposed to be. It's just too weirdly fucked up." He waited a moment as an idea flew into his head, then said, "This is the part where someone always dies, right? Or at least a dead body gets found. Is a dead body going to show up here pretty damn soon, like within the next few paragraphs?" Now he turned to James and practically screamed, "Die, James! Now! Go ahead and die, will you?"

"I'd rather not at the moment, if it's all the same to everyone else."

"Fine, but if this thing ends up a seven-forty-seven over Lockerbie, as in twelve Amazon reviews and a *some nice passages* review from Kirkus, no one can say it was my fault, that's for sure. So don't go blaming me if that's the future of this thing."

"Your dedication to the success of this project is admirable, Rodney."

"Oh, now don't be saying I have no stake in this. I got just as big a stake as either of you guys. It's just that I may be the only one here who's halfway realistic. That's all."

"Thank you, Rodney. Still, despite your well-expressed wishes, I would prefer not to die at the moment, and even were I to do so, I doubt it would further the success of this project. It's not that kind of book. I know it may reflect a certain selfishness on my part, but I'd rather postpone my death to some later date."

This was met with a silence conferring finality. "Wonderful! So, shall we proceed as planned?"

Jonathan Prester didn't discover his true calling in life until the age of sixty-eight, two years after he and his wife, Lydia, had moved to their retirement home at the end of a long dirt road deep in the Green Mountains of Vermont. Their property bordered a Nordic ski club that boasted nearly a hundred miles of groomed trails, so it made sense to take up cross-country skiing as a way to stay in shape through the long winter months. They joined as a family—he, Lydia, and their Cavalier King Charles Spaniel, Scruffy. Although small, Scruffy could keep up with the two of them even on their most ambitious ventures (they also used the trails for hiking in the summer).

The trail idea first came up one cold early morning of that first winter as the three of them trudged the short distance up the dirt road to the entrance of the ski center, skis tucked under their arms and boots slung over their shoulders.

"You know," said Lydia, "it's kind of a pain doing this before and after every ski."

"Yeah, but at least we're close by. Most others have to drive," he answered. Just then his right foot hit a slick spot and his six-foot frame suddenly tilted back before he was able to regain his balance.

"And it's not so safe, either," she said, her right arm instinctually flying out to him, a move that caused the skis tucked under that arm to fall to the ground and clatter across the icy road. He laughed, but Lydia didn't find it so funny. After retrieving her skis, they resumed walking but at a slower pace, and when they reached the entrance to the ski center, Lydia said, "It would be awfully nice to be able to ski right out the front door."

"Yeah, but it's not so far."

She was hoping he'd have picked up the hint by now and might have been gracious enough to bring it up himself, but when he remained silent, she wasted no time in putting it right out there. "If we were to cut down the hillside from our house, then head up the other side of that little canyon, we'd pick up the Skunk Brook trail right before it hits Cool Pool."

"We could, if there was a trail. Do you want to put in a request to the association?"

"No. It's our property. I think we should build ourselves a small connector trail. It couldn't be that hard to do."

Jonathan had to be careful, since he knew exactly who she meant by we. Even though he'd always enjoyed hiking, he'd never had the opportunity or the inclination to make new trails through the wilderness, and had no idea what entanglements might result from a quick commitment. "Good idea," he said, "let's mull on it for a while. Nothing we can do until spring anyway."

Thus he'd successfully parked this chore many months into the future. Funny thing, though. It seemed there was still an inexplicable amount of snow on the ground when Jonathan found himself drawn to spending entire afternoons wandering up and down those wooded hillsides, scouting for the best routes. He traipsed back and forth over the snowbound slopes, stopping to examine any features that either invited or resisted the passage of a trail over its terrain. There were certain stretches that looked like they could very easily be made into a trail—dips, shelves, draws, straight and narrow clearings which he suspected had been used by another generation. Old animal trails most likely, but also very possibly tread by humans of another time.

Two-hundred years ago, the state of Vermont had been briefly overwhelmed by an influx of sheep farmers. The sudden immigration had been triggered by the placement of steep embargoes on wool imported from Ireland and New Zealand. Twenty years later, the embargoes were eased, and by that time, farmers had begun to realize there were much warmer and less rugged parts of the country to raise sheep, or really to do just about any kind of farming. So the vast majority of them left almost as abruptly as they had appeared, leaving behind land reclaimed by nature as true wilderness, with only scattered hints of its previous human occupation – large rocks arranged in mysterious shapes, half-buried rock walls, and streaks through the woods just begging to host part of Jonathan's new trail.

Over the next few months, Jonathan would learn that there was much more to trail-building than just *natural fit*, things like drainage, erosion, gradient, interest, functionality, maintenance, transparency, effect on nearby trees and plants, and difficulty, both in construction and in use. But that knowledge would take time to develop; it was the *natural fit* part that drew him into the woods. Fitting paths onto topographic challenges was like a game to him, always had been, though it took some time for him to remember.

When he was ten, his mom would call him for dinner, and more often than not she'd have to step outside and yell out to the far corner of the backyard where the old sandbox was hidden behind a hedge of magnolias. At first, she suspected the boy was just hiding out, maybe smoking or engaging in some other forbidden activity, but one day she quietly peeked around the hedge and saw that he really was playing in the sandbox. No toys, just running his fingers in the sand. At ten years old and in fifth grade. Even his younger sister had long since given up little kid stuff like sandboxes, but Jonathan had recently begun returning to the abandoned and partially overgrown area.

"Jonny, come in and wash your hands with soap. Who knows what cats have been in that old sand."

"Coming, Mom."

The boy stood up and looked down at his work. Below him stretched the foothills of the Sierra Nevada Mountains, several parallel ridges of increasing altitude and varying steepness. A small ribbon the width of a boy's index finger switchbacked up the first ridge, then rode the crest to preserve elevation before dipping into the higher valley beyond. Resting only briefly along the valley floor, the tiny sandpath gained more elevation by winding in and out of small ravines that fell from the heights of the next ridge over.

"I'll need to finish it tomorrow," he said to himself before turning and running to the house. Yes, he'd be sure to wash his hands.

It was then that he heard what he thought must have been the voice of god. Jonny was not a religious boy, and while he did accompany his mom to Catholic Church every Sunday, this was out of obedience alone. But what he experienced between the sandbox and the patio was more powerful than any previous event in his young life. The moment his right converse lifted from the bed of tanbark surrounding the sandbox to place itself onto the adjacent concrete walkway, god revealed to Jonathan his one true calling in life. It came in a millisecond, but somehow Jonny was able to form a memory of this calling, and he knew right away that it was something very close to what he'd just been playing at—making paths over difficult and uneven terrain.

One moment he was thinking about washing his hands and then suddenly, out of nowhere, he was absolutely convinced of his life's calling. It was indisputable, beyond certain, and who but god could speak with that kind of authority? But why such a strange calling? It didn't make any sense. Such a career was too preposterous to have been dreamed up by Jonny himself; in fact, he'd had no idea that such an occupation even existed, and even if it did, it didn't make any practical sense whatsoever. Building trails out in the woods somewhere? Did people really do that for a living?

As stunning and as certain as this realization had been at the time, it seemed too unreasonable to take seriously, so over time it slowly drifted away, and by the time he needed to give any serious consideration to career choices, it had been discarded altogether. He'd have been embarrassed to even mention it to his high school guidance counselor. Not that it ever left him entirely—you can't forget something like that—but there seemed no way to fit this particular revelation into what he'd been convinced he wanted from life.

What he didn't know was that it wasn't god he'd heard, but rather his own self calling from a later part of his life. He'd experienced what you might call a *lost moment*, had caught the faint rumblings of the leading edge of a wave centered on a time after his sixty-eight-year-old self had finally discovered his true calling. This wasn't magic or time travel or some kind of exception to the laws of physics. It was compelled by the laws of physics.

Warning, here comes the presumptuous mumbo-jumbo. We often think of objects as pieces of matter with clearly defined edges, and in the same way we tend to think of moments, or experiences, as pieces of time that are also held in place by impenetrable boundaries. But both matter and time behave more

like waves than like cohesive blocks, and the rising and falling portions of these waves exist beyond the time frame we ordinarily ascribe to these events.

Because the amplitude of the wave rises and drops sharply, and because it's centered on the *event crest* (I may refer to this also as *home* or *now*), we nearly always perceive moments at, or very close to, their home. But moments exist, and are therefore available to be perceived, at any point along that wave; it's just that as you get further and further away from the event crest, the amplitude of the wave becomes very small, as do the chances of it being perceived from such a distance. But a small percentage of such lost moments do get noticed. Their wave nature doesn't just make such perceptions possible; it makes them rare but certain to occur.

What was especially unusual about this particular experience of Jonny's was that it had triggered a memory, a very rare and powerful event. When moments are perceived very far from their homes, they are so short and so faint that the vast majority of them pass by unnoticed. Once in a great while, though, in a mind that is both empty and receptive at just the right time (usually by the very young, the very old, or the very lunatic), the perception will trigger the formation of a memory. Such a memory allows certain aspects of this experience to be retained.

If you haven't already discounted my blathering as total bullshit, you may have noticed that at least one big question remains unanswered, and I will address this (briefly) later on. For now, though, I really do need to get back to the story, since I've already used up more than my allotment of mumbo jumbo time.

The grown-up and retired Jonathan made several false starts in his first project, causing him to re-route the connector trail twice. From this, he learned his first real lesson: before cutting a single limb or pulling up a single fern, take the time to be absolutely sure of the exact route. Walk it a few times on different days. Only then should you begin the actual construction.

Jonathan quickly discovered that it wasn't just the planning and routing that he loved. The exercise of clearing, cutting, moving rocks and boulders, building short stone walls, and sweeping aside branches and leaves, all at his own pace and with as many breaks as he wanted; it was an exercise perfectly matched to his awkward, big-boned physique as a way to build strength, increase flexibility, and challenge his cardiovascular system without putting too much stress on his joints and bones. The trail construction itself was perfectly suited for both mind and body, and he found himself lured to the woods nearly every afternoon. By the end of July, the connector trail requested by Lydia was complete. Winter was on the way, and perhaps Jonathan had gotten it out of his system and would move on to newer hobbies. If only that had been the case.

Chapter 2

By the time the wood guy arrived at the end of November, there had already been several good snows that had laid down a base likely to last until spring. From his office window, Jonathan saw the truck back up the long driveway, so he grabbed his coat and went out to watch over the unloading.

The outside air bit at his nose as he stepped off the short porch below the front door, then he walked quickly to a spot next to the carport and waved the truck over. When he gave the thumbs-up sign, the front end of the cab began to slowly lift until some threshold was reached, at which point the entire load of firewood slid as one onto the ground in a tremendous crash that threw wood chips and sawdust high into the air.

The driver's side door swung open and a man in jeans and a gray jacket approached. "That OK for you?"

"Perfect," said Jonathan.

"Good, because there's no moving it now."

They both looked at the newly created mountain. "Amazing how much a cord of wood really is," said Jonathan. It was his first time ordering firewood, and he'd had no idea what a cord looked like when he'd placed the order over the phone.

The delivery guy was nice enough to agree. "Yup," he said, but he suspected he was dealing with an amateur, newly arrived from out of state, what with the brand-new house at the end of the road.

"Kinda cold so far this year, don't you think?" said Jonathan. "I mean, at least compared to last year, there's been lots of snow."

"Last year wasn't normal for around here. Way too warm and hardly any snow at all. Maybe this year we'll have ourselves a real winter."

Jonathan kicked at one of the logs that had skittered away from the pile during the big dump. "I sure hope so."

"Me too," said the driver. "Come December this old truck turns into a snow plow. Well, I better get along, so if you could get me a check, that'd be great."

Both men got their wish. As expected, December was snowy, with several good storms and no thaws to interrupt a steady accumulation. But the beginning of January brought with it a prolonged event that was unusual even by Vermont standards. For ten straight days, it snowed continuously, all day, every day. It was a very light snow—no storms or wind—just a persistent soft snowfall that never seemed to break. For a while, the ski center's grooming machine worked overtime until, after a few days, a decision was made to leave it be until the sky was no longer a gray sea full of flakes By then, there was a base of eight feet atop the hill, enough to last the season despite the inevitable thaws that would surely come visiting.

For Jonathan and Lydia, the winter meant daily skiing right out the door using the new trail built over the summer. They took advantage of all the nearby groomed tracks, making loops of five miles up and down the Bald Mountain ridge that rose above their own lesser hill. As they built up their endurance, their expeditions took them further and further away from home until one day Scruffy jumped unexpectedly in front of Lydia as she was barreling down a steep section of The Loop, tumbling her into an icy ditch and injuring her ankle.

The injury wasn't too serious, but it did sideline her for a couple of weeks, and during this time, Jonathan also found himself staying home most days. When her doctor cleared the way for more activity, Lydia was reluctant to get right back on the Nordic skis. They still needed the exercise but figured that snowshoeing would be a safer and more sure-footed alternative.

At first, they kept to their routine ski routes, but even though shoeing was permitted, they had to stick to the sides of the trails, and the looks they got from passing skiers made them uncomfortable. To a skier, a snowshoe is nothing more than an instrument used to damage beautifully smooth tracks groomed to perfection. It was on their third outing that they ventured off-trail. A light drizzle the previous day had frozen overnight into a crust just strong enough to keep them floating atop the eight feet of snow that would have ordinarily swallowed them live.

"I think it's OK. It seems to be holding me," Jonathan called back to his wife.

"If it'll hold you, then it'll hold me, so please, lead the way, big strong man."

Then, in unison, they sang, "Big strong man. Big strong man. Lifts heavy things. Just cause he can," and they laughed that both of them should remember it at the same time. Then Jonathan added, "Falls through the ice. Just cause he can."

Despite the support of the icy crust, the first fifty yards were tough going as the two of them clambered over the tops of low branches and ducked beneath higher ones. Jonathan stopped to let his wife catch up, then reached up and lightly shook a pine limb slumped so deeply by its weight of snow that it pointed nearly straight down. The second his hand touched the branch, it sprung free, releasing a huge shower of icy crystals onto both of them.

"You'd better be ready now," warned Lydia. "Two can play this game, and when you least expect it…"

"Oh, are you offering to lead? Please, be my guest. Remember that the ice is thinner next to big rocks and tree stumps."

They shared a look that confirmed there would be no change of leadership. Then Jonathan leaned over to deliver a short peck of a kiss. "Thanks. Isn't this fun, going off-trail?" he asked, moving forward once again.

"Yeah. But do you have any idea where we're going?"

"Details, details," he joked. Then, in a more serious tone, "I know this whole area is still part of Windekind property, but I've never explored it, not even in summer. In fact, I don't remember any of the others talking about what's up here. Eventually, it turns into state park land, but it's a pretty remote part of the park."

Lydia's next step was a bit more forceful, causing her snowshoe to break through the ice and sink two feet into the snow before she was able to recover by leaning back and placing nearly all her weight on her back foot. Slowly, she extricated the fallen shoe from its newly formed crater and placed it safely back onto the ice. "Whoa! Did you see that?"

He turned to see her point proudly to the hole as if it were a bottomless abyss. "Good one."

"So why didn't *you* break through? You still do weigh more than me, right?"

"No doubt, but nothing's guaranteed out here. We're off into the unknown universe beyond the grooming machine and the racing teams…"

"And don't forget the screaming five-year-olds."

"Aw, but they're cute. I don't mind them."

As they continued northward, the trees stepped back to form a natural corridor. Perhaps an old road or path, thought Jonathan, but they'd settled into a quiet interlude and he decided not to share the thought. It was time to experience the wild still alive in these woods, to take in all the wonder for which they'd left the main trail behind. Twice, they stopped to listen to the near-absolute silence.

The third time they stopped, the snow had begun to fall and the sky had disappeared behind the gently falling flakes. Something had changed, and they both felt it. "This is just like those ten days in January," said Jonathan in almost a whisper, reluctant to break the spell. He looked up and saw nothing but snow. It was as if the sky had become something different altogether, as if weather

itself had been paused. There was no wind— even the lightest breezes had been stilled, and no variation to the pace of the falling snow. The sky shed itself, continuously and uniformly, until the sky became the falling snow and the falling snow became the sky. There was no way to distinguish any difference. Nothing but white sky broken into slowly falling pieces of itself. Even the light seemed to remain unchanged. In those ten days, Jonathan had seen no sunrises, no mornings or afternoons. Just an endless white sky falling lightly through the air.

Lydia was first to break the silence. "This is creepy."

"I know."

"There's something about this place that's giving me the spooks." When she got no answer, she continued. "I mean, look over there," she said, pointing her ski pole off to their left.

He squinted, but it was hard to make anything out in all the snow. "What is it?"

"Over there, see the cliffs?"

"Oh yeah. They are pretty steep. We should go explore them."

"No!" she exclaimed, then in a calmer voice, "Those dark spots in the cliff, especially that one near the very bottom. Do they look like caves to you?"

"Could be. There's an easy way to find out. C'mon."

"No. Jonathan, animals live in caves like that, and we know there are bears around, so can we turn around now? It's been a great snowshoe, but I'm ready to head back to Skunk Brook."

Her husband stared at the dark spots but couldn't tell what they were. In any event, Lydia's intentions couldn't have been any clearer, so he followed behind as she retraced their steps back to the trail.

Snow conditions quickly changed, but they found they much preferred the solitude and beauty of the new route they'd begun, and even though stomping down the snow initially took a lot of work, once it was packed it became easier to both follow and traverse, and over the next couple of weeks they returned frequently, each time pushing the trail just a little bit further into the unknown.

Chapter 3

25

They've been coming up this way for the past few weeks, the two of them. And to tell you the truth, I'm a little worried about it. There's only me left, plus the littles, and I know everything above the high road has been beaten back. There's not even small game left up there anymore. And if it weren't for small game — the very smallest of game—I wouldn't still be alive. It's pathetic, really. I know the eyes of those who ruled these mountains since the beginning are looking down at me, and I'm ashamed of what I've become, scavenging for pathetic little measlies to hunt and eat. The worst part is that I'm forced to go through all the motions of the complete and sacred catamount attack just to nab a rabbit the size of my paw. More than just embarrassing, it's a betrayal to all who came before me, but my body knows no other way to get food, and that's what the littles need most right now. The ancient ones looking down must be disgusted that the elaborate attack ritual developed over millennia and capable of taking down a buffalo or perhaps even a bear, should now be wasted on tiny defenseless creatures I am forced to eat just to survive.

I suspect even the Other can't hunt with the same poise and strength as a catamount. When I was very young, I came across the remains of a kill that was unlike any I'd seen before or since. It's hard to know for sure because the bones were covered with catamount scent, but there was also a faint underlying scent of Other. So maybe it really was one of us that did it, but I also remember being chased away as I approached those remains, and all the other cats kept their distance as well. It was as if the Other carried a threat that could rise from the bones of their dead. It was then I learned that the Other was unlike any other creature and must be avoided at all costs.

It's the *me* that remembers these things as I emerge more frequently from the safety of our small den. It knows that as winter deepens, the littles will only continue to grow hungrier, and small prey will increasingly take to ground. Before long, my teats will be nothing more than dried-out nubs, and the weight of the *me*'s decision grows heavier with each passing day.

26

Chapter 4

From Andersen's Standard Manual of Trail Building:

Beginnings and Ends

Care should be taken to assure that the trail is especially recognizable and clearly marked at its entrance and for the first hundred yards. This will provide the hiker with the reassurance needed to confidently stick to the path, even if latter portions may not be quite so easily distinguishable. The effect can generally be achieved by exaggerating somewhat the standard practices of trail building described elsewhere in this guide. For example, if low plants are cleared to a width of three feet along the main portion of the path, they should be cleared to a width of five feet along the first hundred yards. If overhead limbs are normally clipped to a height of nine feet (as would be the case for a ski or snowshoe trail), they should be clipped to a height of eleven feet at the trail's beginning. Additionally, curves or bends should be minimized, and sharp curves avoided altogether. Users should be able to easily spot the trail's entrance, and the first hundred yards should give the user confidence that he/she has indeed found the path.

Author's Notes:

While this practice makes sense for public trails that are intended to accommodate a lot of foot traffic, one has to fully consider the nature of the user, as Andersen puts it, and I will generally stick with his terminology in my own comments. If the trail is meant for a much more limited group of users, then his advice here won't work very well. If, in fact, the trail is meant as an alternate to a main route, to be used by very few people (maybe as few as five to ten) as a means to avoid the more crowded routes, then an entirely different approach to *beginnings* is required. Just to be clear, I am talking of narrow, single-track routes that may, for example, provide a much more intimate wilderness experience for just one or a few snowshoers who wish to avoid the wide, groomed ski trails that play host to large groups of skiers racing around every bend.

For this type of trail, it is necessary to do the exact opposite of what Andersen recommends; that is, you want to hide the trail entrance as much as possible while still maintaining the key elements of a good trail. In fact, it will likely be necessary to compromise these elements to some extent in order to achieve the desired camouflage necessary to prevent unwanted use by passers-by. One technique I have found especially useful is to avoid removing small saplings at the entrance, and instead wind the trail along a circuitous route around small trees and low brush that would normally have been removed. A long, cleared straight-away branching off from a main route is sure to extend invitations to those you specifically want to keep off the trail. Aside from this, my advice is to do the exact opposite of what Andersen recommends (ie clip branches at a *lower* height, clear ground plants to a *lesser* width, etc.). You may also place a large rock or log which may appear to block the way but in reality can easily be skirted. In fact, such an obstacle can serve as an easy way to locate the trail for those who have been clued in.

Of course, for those seeking true isolation, going cross-country with no trail at all can be the best option, but only in the proper conditions. Sparse snow cover may hide obstacles, and heavy snow cover can be impossible to wade through. So smaller trails, private and hidden, do serve a purpose for the wilderness explorer. Just be sure to construct them in a manner that will maintain that intimacy.

I found it interesting that, aside from this quick mention related to a trail's entrance, Andersen avoided altogether the critical element of *followability*, or what some have called *ease of distin-*

guishment. He does include it as one of the essential traits, saying in a very general sense that a trail should be easy to follow, but gives no opinion on the matter of degree, a subject that is foremost in the mind of any good trailmaker who takes his craft seriously. Do you want your trail so easy to follow that hikers do so automatically, looking down at their feet the whole time and not bothering to look ahead to make out what may lie ahead? But isn't that a big part of the enjoyment of hiking, constantly scouting ahead, looking for clues as to where the path is headed next? As a trailmaker, you have an obligation to satisfy the hiker's appetite for challenge and curiosity, and this means that the trail should not be too easy to follow, in my opinion.

I am referring specifically to forest trails, but, of course, you are free to consider this guidance in whatever light may come to mind. I am reminded of a study which found ambiguity to be one of the very few traits reliably associated with artistic masterpieces. It's not that every ambiguous painting is a masterpiece, but it's hard to find a true masterpiece that lacks an undeniably intriguing element of uncertainty. While none of my trails will ever be mistaken for a Vermeer, trail builders should still consider challenge, ambiguity, and yes, even the slight possibility that their users might become entirely lost, at least momentarily. A result that some would see as evidence of utter failure on the part of the trailmaker might very well be a situation secretly

longed for in the far reaches of the serious hiker's brain. Isn't the greatest adventure of all to be lost in the wilderness? While that's certainly not our objective, we do have a responsibility to restrain ourselves from making the trail so obvious that any possibility of such an occurrence is completely eliminated. That's just my own opinion. There's no correct answer here, and much depends on the type of hiker for whom you're making the trail. But the degree to which, and the distance at which, a path can be distinguished should be planned and executed by any good trailmaker.

From *A Field Guide to Wild Animals of the Northeast*:

A powerful predator once roamed the lush green forests and mountains of Vermont— the eastern cougar, locally known as the catamount. These large, nimble felines hunted among the sugar maples and white pines, helping maintain healthy ecosystems for thousands of years. As apex predators, catamounts kept deer and other prey populations in check, preserving the balance of nature.

When European colonists began settling the Vermont wilderness in the eighteenth century, they viewed the native catamounts as threats. As livestock farming grew and wilderness was cleared for farms and villages, conflicts arose. Bounties were soon placed on the heads of catamounts, encouraging settlers to shoot them on sight or trap them for reward money. The combination of active hunting and rapid habitat loss devastated Vermont's cougars over the coming decades.

Sightings grew rare. The last confirmed catamount killed in the state met its end near Barnard, Vermont, in 1881, though unconfirmed sightings continued for a few decades after. Still, the population was never able to recover. In 2018, nearly 150 years after that last confirmed local killing, the eastern cougar was officially declared extinct across its entire native range, including Vermont. A creature that once defined Vermont's forests had vanished, with only paw prints remaining fossilized in the state's memory.

Heard recently in Vermont conversations:

"I saw one 10 years ago on West Jamaica Rd in Jamaica. Came up the bank of Ball Mountain Brook and crossed in front of me. I couldn't believe it at first, but the tail was unmistakable. It leapt 15 feet deep into the woods. Nothing has a tail like that except a Catamount."

"I one hundred percent saw one in my backyard a couple of years back. Got a Bigfoot quality picture, and still have it. Its tail was long. It was about fifty feet away. It looked at me. Figured it would either walk away or I was dead, so got the best photo I could."

"I saw one walking through my backyard (Chittenden County), it was almost midnight, and one of the trees in our backyard was lit up for Christmas. Originally, I thought it was a bobcat or lynx (was easily two times the size of a normal cat). It had a long tail, so I really do think it was a catamount, but maybe a juvenile. I followed the tracks the next morning.

Chapter 5

Maintaining a snowshoe trail amounted to no more than using it frequently enough to keep the narrow trench of packed snow from getting lost beneath fresh snowfalls. It was especially important to do so after a big storm, even in the middle of a storm if it was the kind of event that lasted more than a day. In early April, though, the base began to melt from below, revealing surprising obstacles they had never guessed lay beneath their well-planned-out route—fallen trees, large boulders, and huge roots that emerged from the dirt, lay above ground for a stretch, then dove underground once again. Some of these created giant loops perfectly shaped to trip an inattentive hiker.

As April turned to May, the summer forest once again emerged, looking exactly as it had the year before, as if winter had never happened. This was when Jonathan cursed himself for not having better marked the route. With the track so well laid out and so easy to follow, he had just assumed that, come summer, they would remember the way, but the first few snowless visits to the area resulted in Jonathan frequently getting completely turned around, and even lost at times. Eventually, he would always find the general track, but he also realized that an all-season trail (which is what he and Lydia both wanted) couldn't follow the exact route of a snowshoe trail due to the underlying topography and features of the ground itself. So he started making a few necessary changes, on his own. He should have consulted with his wife because it really was theirs together, but he got a bit carried away, and besides, he wanted to surprise her with all the work he'd been doing.

And he absolutely loved doing it. There was so much more than just cutting limbs and ripping out ferns and small plants. Moving rocks, finding narrow passages through fallen trees; it seemed each ten-yard stretch had its own unique challenge. But the part he liked best involved stacking rocks. Fitting them together in just the right way to form steps, or short walls to support the path on steep slopes, and sometimes to form part of the trail itself. He loved every part of it—the searching and finding of rocks just the right size and shape, excavating the foundation on which the formation will rest, then fitting them all together into the desired architecture. Finally, there was the rearrangement and reformation, as he questioned if this one rock would be better off over there, and if so, then this other stone could fill in the gap left by the previous rock. This could go on for quite a while, and before he knew it, it would be dinnertime.

The next day, he asked Lydia if she wanted to look at the work he'd been doing on what they had started calling *the snowshoe trail*.

"Sure. You've been spending a lot of time out there, that's for sure."

"I know. It's a lot of work to make it into something we can use in the summer too. We can use it as an alternate to Dead River since it kind of parallels it. Want to see the map?"

She wasn't nearly as interested in the map as he was but knew his obsession with maps went way back, to the time they first met, in fact. So she wasn't going to deny him this pleasure. "Yes," she said. "Let's see where this thing is going."

He pulled it up online and they gazed at it for a few minutes. It had all the groomed trails, and he'd added both the new connector trail as well as *the snowshoe trail* in dotted lines.

"This is just projected, of course. So far it only goes to about here," he said, pointing to a spot about a third of the way from the start.

"You know, there are others here who would love to use this, especially in winter. Nicole, Jennifer, Matt…"

"Hold on. Let's get a little more work done first before we go announcing it to everyone."

There was a protracted silence, and Jonathan tried to brush it aside. "Shall we go, then?"

Lydia hesitated, then said, "Have you gotten the LLC's approval for that? I mean, this one is on communal property."

There was no answer, and Lydia didn't need one since she sat in on all LLC meetings and knew for sure that he had never mentioned it. So they started out in silence down the hillside to the connector trail, slippery with the mud of three previous days of cold rain but now glistening in the welcome sun. They turned right on Skunk Brook and soon arrived at the beginning of the snowshoe trail, summer edition.

READER: *The following chapter and accompanying photos describe the snowshoe trail. While this may be of interest to outdoor enthusiasts and lovers of Vermont landscapes, it does not contribute directly to the plot itself. If you wish to skip this section, please proceed directly to the blue rectangle at the bottom of page forty-one.*

"What the fuck?"

"Damn, and he'd been good for so long. I told you he wouldn't like this."

"Yeah, you got that right. What the fuck is this all about? You're telling them to just skip over part of the book? This is totally apeshit!"

"Calm down, Rodney. Yes, we know it's kind of new and different, but we just wanted to give a heads up to those readers who aren't really into descriptions of woods and trails. So they can skip ahead a little bit and still pick up the plot."

"I thought the only people reading this were into woods and trails and shit. You guys have lost it."

"Well, they wouldn't be into shit, so I agree with that part of your assessment," said James.

"Ha," laughed Rodney. "I've got an even better idea. At the very end of the book, let's put a picture of a big monkey face, and on the very first page you tell them that if they want to just skip the entire fucking book, all they have to do is proceed directly to the bottom of page three hundred and fucking seven!"

"I really think you're overreacting, Rodney. Why don't we ask the author what he thinks?"

"It doesn't matter to me one way or another," said the author. "I know my fans won't skip ahead. And everyone will probably look at the pictures."

"So if it doesn't fucking matter, then don't put it there in the first place. This would be hilarious if it wasn't so fucking fucked!"

"*Fucking fucked.* That's good. Can you string three in a row and still keep it grammatically correct?"

Rodney didn't answer, so apparently he'd said his fill for the time being.

Chapter 6

Are you still here? If so, and if you haven't skipped ahead like so many of the others, we've got something a bit special lined up for you. Ordinarily, the author would have described this trail himself, but we've arranged to have the trail reviewed by the legend of trail critics, none other than William C. Hemsmeth himself. Yes, it's true that this NYC-based columnist who has been a regular contributor to journals such as Nature, Smithsonian, and National Geographic, did retire several years ago. But our persistence, as well as the deep pockets of this publisher…

"Deep pockets? Are you kidding me? How much did this cost us?"

"Not now, Rodney. Later, OK?"

Anyway, as I was saying, William C. Hemsmeth has agreed to come out of retirement to provide us with a brief review of this trail, shown below. Now aren't you glad you didn't skip this part?

Trail: Currently called *The Snowshoe Trail*

Length: 0.8 miles, 1.6 miles with return.

Trailhead Location: Unable to disclose, but northern Vermont, 1400 ft elevation

Trailmaker: Anonymous. We will refer to him/her as "Ki".

Given the location, how could this trail be anything other than delightful in any season, despite the given name that implies only a snowshoe trail. But I hiked it in autumn and it was certainly very negotiable.

This is Ki's second trail, following his debut last year with the *Connector Trail*, which I also had a chance to hike (let's just say it has many opportunities for improvement that one typically sees in debuts by amateur trail makers. A debut at age 67! I should say, a veritable Grandma Moses). I normally do not review amateur work, but in this case I simply could not turn down what they were offering me.

"Fuckin'-a"

Did I hear something? Should I go on? OK, I've been told to continue, so let's get right to the trail itself. It begins from an established ski trail, and I can guarantee you would not find it unless given directions, since it ducks sharply to the left, then makes nearly a full circumnavigation of a fir sapling before opening into a long straightaway lined with small firs on one side. It is such a gradual climb, and is so perfectly straight, that I suspect Ki has utilized an old wagon or sheep trail. It makes sense to do so, and allows easy

hiking up to a junction with what appears to be still another previously used corridor. The long hallways finally end at the top of a rise, where the trail swings right and dances back and forth through the trees. This is an especially wonderful section of this trail, maybe my favorite. It descends slightly as it weaves, then bears left before swinging right, apparently to avoid proximity to some tall cliffs and what may be animal

Den, visible from trail

Close up of den

homes embedded therein. This may be the suspected location of the cat den that I believe is referred to later in this book. I was asked to continue the description further, though, since it was uncertain specifically where certain *encounters* might take place, so let us continue.

Here is where things start to become darker and more serious. Amidst large stones and overgrown roots covered in thick moss, the trail makes its way steeply uphill through a much deeper and more mature forest than seen earlier. The canopy must be extremely thick, with the forest nearly entirely coniferous at this point, but the trail is easy enough to follow, and the switchbacks handle the grade nicely. The route generally does a good job of following rises and small hillocks to make its way forward, thus avoiding mush and mud, and also keeping the hiker up high on firm ground.

After the switchbacks, it emerges into an open glade of birch and maples. The clouds that seems to have been shadowing the previous stretch ascend and once again we are in cheerful surroundings. Beech trees have spoken for every gap left behind by the maples and birches. The forest floor is awash with maple vines aspiring to someday become trees and small beech trees which, because of their extreme youth, have a more delicate appearance than you would ever think of ascribing to a birch tree. The leaves are soft and light green, and dapple the hillsides quite gracefully.

A few technical points: on my return, I must have taken a wrong turn because I ended up on some kind of alternate path through some very wet marshland. Some additional attention to marking at this spot would help avoid future lost souls wandering around the marshes, unless, of course, that is exactly what Ki had in mind. From some of his previous statements, I wouldn't put it past him.

On the positive side, Ki has done a good job of keeling off the stumps of adjacent trees to protect eyes and heads and other such vital organs, and he has also taken care to mark any particularly nasty obstacle that he hasn't yet had the time to get rid of. It seems the trailmaker is not so worried about you getting lost in the wetlands, but will make every effort to save you from unexpectedly tripping over a stubbed foot.

All in all, a decent start of a new trail by a debut trailmaker never before reviewed in a major journal. I'd have used the term *promising* but for the fact that Ki is really too old to properly carry such a designation. And that should just top the seven hundred words stipulated in the contract, not that anybody's counting. Signing out from what is likely to be my last review, this has been William Hemsmeth.

Here is an example of the many emerging roots in the area. The trailmaker was wise to let this one be.

Some courteous clipping

The trailmaker was a bit exuberant about marking the sides of the trail

*Trail's entrance, in keeping with the trailmaker's **built to be overlooked** philosophy*

Chapter 7

"OK. So, that's about it for tonight's agenda."

"Wow, you mean we're actually going to finish before nine o'clock?"

"Looks that way. Anyone have anything else they want to add to the agenda or just talk about?"

There was a short silence, but before the moderator could ask for a motion to adjourn, a voice spoke up. It was Bill.

"Hey Matt, it's Bill."

"Bill, you making a motion to adjourn?"

"Uh, no. Sorry. There actually is one more thing I'd like to bring up, if that's all right."

"Sure, go right ahead. There's plenty of time."

Now Bill hesitated, as if gathering his thoughts. "I've been sitting on this for a while because I was really hoping Jonathan would have brought it up, but it doesn't look like that's going to happen. And it's no big deal, but it is something to do with the by-laws, so I thought we should discuss it here."

"Sure, go right ahead," said Matt, hearing in his mind all of the silent *I just knew we couldn't end on time even just this once* thoughts bouncing around the Zoom call.

"It has to do with doing work or making improvements on common land. My understanding is that this kind of activity requires LLC approval ahead of time. Am I getting that right?”

There were a few sounds of consent heard before Matt said, “Yes. That’s correct.”

“And wouldn’t building trails on common land fall under that statute?”

Now that Jonathan knew what this was all about, he unmuted himself and spoke. “Guilty as charged. I’m sorry, everyone. Bill’s right; I have been working on a trail recently, mainly as a snowshoe trail, so I’m not doing a lot of heavy-duty stuff like building walls or stairs or anything like that. I thought that I’d mentioned it to folks last winter when Lydia and I were using it a lot. In fact, I think Nicole came with us one time. But you’re absolutely right; I should have formally gotten approval before I started doing anything.”

“I’m not so sure,” said Matt. “If you’re not actually building anything, does it fall under the by-law?”

Bill’s voice had a defensive edge to it now. “Yes, he’s building a trail. Not just a snowshoe trail, which is just tracks on snow, but an all-season trail, with plants cleared, tree limbs cut, sections where dirt has been dug from the hillside to level the path, that kind of stuff. I think we should all be OK with a project like that if it’s built on common land, that’s all.”

“And I agree. It was my mistake, really, and I’m not arguing the point at all. Tell you what, I’ll send some pictures and a map to everyone, and in the meantime, I’ll stop all work. Then we can discuss it at the next meeting and you guys can decide.”

Angie was the next to speak, and her words seemed to reflect the general opinion because they were followed by thumbs-up signs and very little subsequent discussion. “I think that’s very gracious of you, Jonathan. I doubt it’s going to be any problem at all, and I hate to see your work get interrupted, but technically, Bill is correct, so I agree with what you’ve offered to do.”

Jonathan was pleased with the consensus, and while he did provide the map and photos as promised, he didn't pause the trail's northward push. After all, winter was right around the corner. What bothered him the most was how easily Bill had discovered the trail, and he pondered possible ways of improving the camouflage.

From The Montpelier Times Argus, Aug 30, 2022:

Recent reports of big cat sightings have captured the imagination of local residents eager to know what species of wild felines might be living in Waterbury.

Though the infamous catamount was officially declared extinct in 2018, several people spotted big cats that they thought to be mountain lions on Ripley Road two weeks ago, as related in posts on Front Porch Forum.

One, Waterbury resident Jeff Kilgore's sister-in-law, came across the cats while walking a dog on Ripley Road on a Monday morning. They were "very large, light tan, with long legs, and long white-tipped tails," Kilgore wrote, relaying the account.

The other, a utility worker checking the meter on Ripley Road, claimed he saw "two mountain lions" when describing the encounter to Ripley Road resident Russell Snow. The worker was in his truck when the cats crossed the road in front of the dog-walker, Snow said. He honked his horn to scare them off, and the cats made their way into Snow's yard.

"At around 9:30," Snow said, "I was outside working and I heard the horn blow. And somebody hollering. And then he drove up into my yard to read the meter. He said there were two, he called them mountain lions."

The cats passed by, moving west through Snow's property.

"This is a natural wildlife corridor coming down off of the Worcester Range headed over towards the Green Mountain Range. We have a lot of bear traffic through here, and deer,"

Snow said. "I did not see the cats, but I did talk to the guy. He was very shook up. I'll tell you that."

The Vermont Department of Fish & Wildlife accepts reports of potential big cats using an online form at anrweb.vt.gov/FWD/FW/FurbearerReportingForm.aspx. They have not received any reports of large cats in Waterbury so far. In any case, identification without a photo is a challenge, according to Fish & Wildlife officials. Mountain lions are not likely to pass through Vermont, according to Fish & Wildlife biologist Chris Bernier. "Having been doing this since 1994, I have yet to have had a definitive, documented, indisputable, verifiable sighting of a mountain lion," Bernier said.

Photo by Gerard Lacz

Chapter 8

I know what you're thinking. You're thinking, how can a catamount be so smart and use all these words like it's human. You're thinking, boy this particular catamount is awfully smart and sophisticated. Yes, it's true that my words have been given to me, but I use them only to describe things I really do know.

You think just because I don't have a fancy name for snow that I don't know what snow is? Ha! I spend more time in the snow than twelve of you combined. For five months of the year I live entirely in snow. So if you've thought about it just a little bit, then you've already realized that yes, I know snow and I know it well, better than you. And you think that because I can't say the word *road* that I don't know what a road is? Or a trail? I mean, up here they're dirt, but you might be surprised to know that I'm also quite familiar with the hard ones further down the mountain. I get around, let me tell you. Yeah, I know every road and trail in my territory and to do that you have to know what a road is, right? So when I start talking about the Others and how they started their trail from the lowest road, three leaps from the creek, then you really should believe me and not just laugh away the things I have to say because I'm just some dumbshit animal. OK?

I mean, we have to make an agreement right here that I know what I'm talking about, and I'll tell you only the truth. You may not yet have a full understanding of what a catamount really is, and how a catamount really thinks and feels. But as for what I tell you here, it's only what I do see, hear, and feel. I don't pretend to know things which are beyond me. So if we're to walk any further together, we need to have this agreement: You will not think me a bullshitter, and I will not bullshit. Really. Despite what you'll read about in later chapters, and despite how I may challenge your understanding of the true nature of catamounts, you have to take my word for it. Because if we can't agree on that, then you should walk away right now, and I should turn and make two giant leaps for the safety of the forest.

So please don't question that I know these things. It's the way I know them that is different from you. You know them in your head, and I know them in my body. My body knows and my body remembers, not just everything I've seen and learned in my life but everything that's been placed into my body by millennia of catamounts before me. You think this impossible, for my body to know so much? Have you heard Vladimir Ashkenazy play the entire Emperor concerto without a thought in his head? (No? That's OK; either have I, but I have it on good authority). His fingers know every nuance and shade of every note. The written notes are there only as prompts should his fingers somehow lose their way. So why do you question that a catamount's body is capable of knowledge more complex than you might have presumed?

This afternoon, for the first time in two months, I leave the den because I hear it coming and I want to watch, from a distance. It's still there now, repeatedly bending over to rip out small plants, but it doesn't eat them. Instead, it tosses them aside. Is it leaving them there to eat later? Does it know that bending over like that, with such predictable timing, makes it a ridiculously easy target? Occasionally, it whacks above at a tree branch or bends one back and forth until it falls to the ground. Then it just tosses the branch into the woods. Whatever it's doing, it remains upright and utterly unafraid. At odd times, it stops and looks around, but it doesn't appear to be scouting for prey. It acts and moves as if it's the top predator, and I have to respect that, even though it's size, strength, and movement suggest an easy kill. Maybe that's what Ud was trying to tell me, that the Other must have a hidden and deadly weapon. There aren't very many of those kinds of animals around here, but they do exist, and my body not only knows they exist but also knows the best way of dealing with them. It's a built-in mechanism. First of all, we take a lot of time, days even, to carefully observe any animal that we've never killed before. We know to be wary of camouflaged threats. Snakes, skunks, and porcupines are examples of these kinds of animals. The technique is to watch first, then approach slowly.

While still at least two leaps away, it's important to make a quick move to *prompt a reaction,* so if it really does have a hidden weapon, it will deploy it prematurely, while you are still at a safe distance. While it's true that such a move reveals your location and spoils the immediate hunt, getting the information is more important. Then, if no hidden threat is triggered, you can hunt the prey in the usual manner.

That's probably the reason Ud warned me off the Other that day; he was trying to tell me that they're off-limits because they have hidden weapons. But there was something else in his eyes, a feeling, a deeper fear of the Other itself that went beyond just our own danger from its immediate response to an attack. Because Ud's look was not routine. It wasn't a reminder to test for the threat at two leaps. It said we need to leave, now, and never since have I come within three giant leaps of the Other.

Here is where even the words so generously given me fail, because it's something I feel and it's something unclear that I don't understand, but it's there nonetheless, this sense that the Other is a mystical creature that can strike back from beyond the kill. Long ago, when Ud and I saw a lone Other high up on Bald Hill and I began to stalk it since I was very hungry, Ud looked hard at me and his eyes told me there was something different about the Other. That yes, I could stalk the Other, and maybe even make a kill, but doing so would bring terrible things down on the entire pride, that the Other would return to take its vengeance and that the vengeance would hurt not just me, but all of us. I know this sounds crazy, and like I say, I don't understand this feeling, but

it's enough to make me hesitate, and a predator can't be successful with even the slightest bit of hesitation. Since then, and until today, I've never even silently watched an Other, much less stalked one. But today I am watching, from several leaps away, yes, but I *am* watching, and it's only because of the awful sounds of my starving littles.

Last night I dreamed of cows. Small, tall cows.

Chapter 9

Jonathan was excited to show Lydia the newest part of the trail.
She was the only one he could show it off to because he was
supposed to be pausing his work, but she was also the only one
he really wanted to show it to. She always appreciated trailwork,
and they would snowshoe on it together in just a few months.

She was already gushing before they reached the new section.

"This is really great, Jon. It's so much better than before."

"Thanks, but all I did here was brush aside leaves and re-route
where it used to go in the swamp."

"This way is so much better. Look, you did more," she tapped
her toe on the top of a small ridge of rocks he'd made. "And
here too," she added, walking over to a spot where he'd filled in
a hole with two rocks he'd moved from higher up the hillside.
"You've done a lot of work."

"Yeah, I guess. Clean up stuff. But up here is the new part." He
stopped at the top of several switchbacks that wound up a dark,
heavily wooded draw and pointed ahead to where the path dipped
up and down as it intersected a family of birch trees.

"It's beautiful."

"Wait, where's Scruffy? Is he still with us?"

"He's right here, literally right next to your legs."

Jonathan looked down and twisted his head around to see the

dog. He should never have worried about Scruffy getting lost. Every time he thought the dog might have disappeared, it turned out he was so close as to be nearly invisible. "C'mon," he said, "there's not much more, but I'll show you where it ends for now."

The end was clearly marked by a large downed tree falling directly across the presumed continuation of the route. Big enough to have to climb over. They both sat for a few minutes and listened to the woods, looking around in all directions. Finally, Lydia broke the silence.

"So which way does it go from here?"

"I'm not sure. You want to explore a little and try to find a good way?"

Lydia looked at her watch and said, "Not today. I've got to get back for a Zoom call."

"One of your kiddies?"

"Yeah, my seventh grader is starting to skip school again," she said, referring to one of the kids with unsettled home situations she represented in court as a volunteer Guardian Ad Litem. It was a retirement hobby that did a lot more good for the world than making trails out in the middle of nowhere, trails unlikely to be used by more than a handful of hikers and skiers.

"OK," he sighed as they both stood to go their separate ways. "I'm going to investigate alongside this little creek a little further to see what's up there. I'll be home for dinner."

They hugged and exchanged a quick kiss before she started back down the new trail, presenting Scruffy with a difficult situation.

"Looks like he's chosen you," Jonathan called after his wife, and she was quick to reply.

"Keep an eye out, though. Remember that time he kept trying

to switch between us. I wouldn't be surprised if he runs back and forth for the next twenty minutes before he finally makes a decision."

"Will do. At least he's been up this way with me before, so he knows the way home."

With that, Jonathan turned and scouted the hillside that swept down from the top of Cobble Hill to a wall of huge cliffs rising up to his right. The junction between the two formed a small seasonal creek that fed the larger, year-round creek on the other side of the cliffs. Between the creeks rose an immense, rock-guarded mound topped with a mature grove of large fir trees. It was one of the most topographically interesting areas on the property, and it was no accident that the *snowshoe trail* slid by right next to it.

Jonathan made his way up the left side of the creek until the brush became so thick that he knew laying a trail there would be way too time-consuming. He returned to the fallen tree at the end of the current trail and was about to explore a route further to the left, along the side of the slope, but changed his mind. Maybe revisiting the spot where he and Lydia had shared a quiet moment reminded him of how delighted she had seemed with the minor improvements he'd made further down. In any event, he decided to walk back along the existing path and take care of a few spots he knew still needed more work.

As he began to walk slowly downhill, he heard a rustle of leaves that caught his attention. This time of year, that sound is more the norm than the exception. So why had it stopped him in his tracks? Why had he even noticed it at all? He stood very quietly and listened intently. Is it here? Is this the place? He knew it was nearby, the exact location his life would end. He'd been there before. Not a dream but like a dream; not a premonition but like a premonition. It was real, he knew that, but what do you call the memory of something that hasn't happened yet?

The moment passed in silence, and he was still there. It wasn't yet the time, so he continued on his way. At the first switchback, he found Scruffy chugging slowly toward him from the other direction, his panting on serious overdrive.

"Scruffy, you poor dog," he said, bending down to smooth down the hair atop the dog's curiously shaped head. Scruffy responded by stretching up and placing his paws on Jonathan's knees. "Oh, I know what you want," he said, then bent over to vigorously scratch his lower back. "That's what you want, is a good, hard, butt scratch."

The dog suddenly abandoned the absolute nirvana of a back scratch for a bound into the upslope woods, his continuous barking peppered with occasional growls that surely pushed the limits of a Cavalier King Charles Spaniel's ability to be taken seriously as a threat.

"Scruffy, get back here. C'mon, there's nothing out there. You'll just tire yourself out even more." Of course, Scruffy, being deaf, only escalated his barrage of warnings called out to an empty forest. Finally, Jonathan had to walk out and grab his collar to pull him back to the trail. There, he squatted down and tried to calm a dog with a history of barking at nothing. At one time, Jonathan theorized that these assaults on stretches of innocuous woodlands were an attempt to compensate for his deafness; being unable to hear the approach of danger, he was compelled to warn away all possible unheard threats. Whatever the cause, his propensity to go charging out at nothing was becoming quite an annoyance.

It took a good ten minutes until Scruffy was calm enough to settle into his habit of tagging along quietly, and before long Jonathan was fully engaged in supporting a small section of trail that appeared vulnerable to heavy rain. Just the right rocks had to be found, a task complicated by the ineligibility of any rock already serving a useful purpose in its current location. Then came the arrangement of large rocks, followed by the smaller ones, and finally by any additional needed support (earth-shaping, logs, etc.). By the time he neared completion of this mini-project, the sun was low, and he could tell it was time to head back. So he gathered his tools, took one last survey of the work he'd done, then looked around for Scruffy.

"Scruffy?"

He looked in all directions, but there was no sign of the small dog. He nearly called out again in a louder voice before remembering he was deaf. Calling out to a dog is such a natural thing that even with this knowledge, the urge to yell out to him was nearly impossible to restrain. But he knew where Scruffy had gone—back home to Lydia. This happened more often than not when Jonathan spent time in a single location. So he took one last look around and took off at a quick pace, determined to make it home by dinnertime.

Early on, I hear the Other approach once more, this time two of them sharing their sing-song calls that are so unlike the sounds of any other animal. They walk along the same path that comes uncomfortably close to our small den. After they pass, I wait long enough to give each of my littles a quick tongue bath, then I look long and hard at each of them, one at a time, with the sternest eyes a catamount mother can show to her young. They know exactly what this means; they were born knowing it: *I'm leaving you now and while I'm gone you're to remain absolutely silent and are not to leave the den under any circumstances.* I don't need words to tell them this, and they don't need thoughts to understand. Their bodies know. It's actually a very efficient way of communicating.

I creep quietly from the den and make one long leap to a nearby tree for cover. There I stay put for a long time, hesitant to move any closer to the Other, questioning my decision to watch. This is a step I've never taken before by myself; only one time have I been so bold as to watch an Other for any length of time, and that was long ago, when I had Ud by my side. It was different then because we had accidentally stumbled into their area. We watched, but only to assure a safe distance was kept between us and them. This time I watch because watching is the first step of any catamount hunt.

I steal through the trees, moving continuously uphill and sniffing the various holes in the ground and cracks in the boulders, ever alert for even the smallest prey to free me from this dangerous game I'm playing, but the foxes and bobcats have picked the area clean. Despite our status as master hunters, foxes and bobcats are much better suited for nabbing the small ground squirrels and moles that large cats traditionally have had no need to pursue. Today, though, I'd gladly take a squirrel or two if there were any to be had.

I stop on a narrow shelf halfway up the slope that makes for a good lookout. It has a clear line of sight to the two Others, who are resting on a fallen tree, so I lie on the leaves with my paws stretched in front of me, observing them as they exchange calls to each other. I'm still not sure of my plan of attack, and my legs stop for a moment, remembering the cardinal rule of all predators: even the smallest hesitation will spoil the chase. There can be no questions or second thoughts; all prey is too fast and too smart to be caught by an uncertain predator, even if that predator is a catamount.

The two of them stand and begin retracing their steps in my direction, continuing on until they pass the den. The smaller is walking ahead and the larger following closely behind. As soon as I'm confident that this new movement is a course reversal and not just a short investigation into some nearby point of interest, I know I might be spotted if I don't quickly relocate. Their move surprises me since they stopped for just a short while, and never did reach the upper canyon where the larger one has recently been spending most of it's time. In a bit of a panic, I draw my paws in too quickly while at the same time neglecting to retract my claws. The harsh sound breaks a jagged hole the quiet of the morning, and for a moment I'm sure it will give me away. In fact, one of them does stop abruptly and look around in all directions, so I do what cats do best: maintain perfect silence and perfect stillness for as long as necessary, and then some. Other predators have neither the mental patience nor the physical strength to match us cats at this game. For those long seconds, it feels as if all my legs are quivering with fear. Invisible, I know, but to me it feels as if the ground itself is shaking. I'm as much afraid of what I might do as what the Other might do.

You see, for all my boasting about muscle memory being so convenient and efficient, there's a downside to it as well. Because my body and my decision-making are pretty much the same thing, the *me* part can be left out altogether. (Yes, there is a *me* in here, and even though it's in its infancy, it knows that I'm more than just a bundle of pre-programmed neural reflexes. And the *me* is awfully scared right now because it knows that it has no say at all in most of my actions. For example, once my body detects that it's been spotted by prey, it jumps straight into the *chase and kill* sequence. The *me* can't stop a reaction that's hard-wired into all catamounts and probably all predators. And the truth of the matter is that the *me* is not ready to take down the Other. The *me* doesn't want that at all. And it's not only because the Other might possess a hidden danger. There's more to it than that. Its mysterious and graceful movements and calls seem to have an unknown purpose behind them, and I have to admit that the *me* has grown to like the Other and doesn't want this to happen. But it does happen. I know it. I've seen it. Not a dream, not a hunch, but something real. What's the word for a memory of something that hasn't happened yet?

I'm still here. And the other is still here. We are safe, for now. But the time is close, I can tell. So I amuse myself by watching all the silly things the other does with the ground. And I enjoy it; it grows a certain endearment inside my heart that turns to poison every time I remember what has to happen.

The Other seems to like things to be flat and gradual. For quite a while, it devotes its full attention to a very small section of the forest floor, doing nothing but stomping on dirt. It looks to be fresh dirt that has recently been placed there in quantity, and after spreading it out with his feet, it begins a strange stomping activity. The foot pounding continues endlessly, and the only reason I can think of for it is that the Other likes things flat. So it's all to make the ground flat. But despite the lengths of time spent this way, I watch it all, and I could have continued watching it all day long. In some odd way, I find it mesmerizing.

There's something very special and beautiful in how the Other moves and the things it does. The way it's able to smash away overhead branches and stack rocks in elegant lines next to trails, and the way it spends so much time looking for those rocks, choosing only the misfits. It's got such a tremendous knowledge of the land as well as a willingness, even an eagerness, to care for it. To be the trailmaker. That's what the Other is, after all: the trailmaker. And in all these millennia of years, no other animal has stepped forward to try and take its place. But then again, who else really wants to be the trailmaker? It's not like we're a bunch of idiot moo-cows out here who need to be told where to place our paws. The Other is really the only one who seems to have a need for them, although I do have to admit that the Other's trails are very good for one thing: speed. If you need to relocate quickly from one part of the forest to another, there's nothing like an Other trail to get you there in a hurry. And those wide paths will sometimes attract prey who are trying to escape me, which is a mistake because in an all-out sprint, there is nothing that can outrun a catamount.

As I continue to spy on the Other, I get the sense that it's more than just its intelligence that's affecting the *me*. I get the feeling that it really does love the land, like I love the land. Maybe not in exactly the same way, but we both do love it— that much we share. And it takes such incredible care of the ground. I watch as it spends almost an hour on one tiny patch of dirt on the forest floor. Based on the amount of time and work it spends on such a tiny piece of land, I'm guessing that little patch of dirt must have some serious problems. It actually gets down on its hands and knees to administer aid of an almost intimate nature: digging through the dirt with its bare hands, shaping the loose soil, running its fingers through the leaves to brush them aside. Perhaps they're suffocating the ground in some way. Then it lines the lower side of this patch with big rocks, after which it finally stands up and reaches its long arms up toward the canopy high above. I prepare to switch locations, but when the Other does move, it's in an unexpected direction toward the creek, so I stay

put. After rummaging through the assortment of rocks and boulders in the creek bed, it climbs back up the hill, its arms now full of specially chosen stones which must have the ability to heal the broken spot. These rocks are smaller than the ones it's already laid down, and it places these right next to the bigger ones, on the downslope side. Each placement is pounded down with a larger rock, and dirt is packed in between any openings surrounding this new rock. I find the whole process quite mysterious and utterly fascinating.

Beneath the smaller rocks, it lays down large branches for these stones to lean upon. Then finally—and you won't believe this (it's the kind of thing that makes me think I can never hurt the Other because if I were ever in any trouble, it might be the only one who could save me)—but finally, it breaks off pieces of small, dead sticks and pounds them vertically down into the dirt, to hold up the branches he has just laid down. I'm told these are called stakes, but I'm not entirely sure of their purpose. And all this intensive care it gives to just one very tiny spot of dirt on the forest floor. I ask myself why, and I can only believe it must love everything out here: the trees and the leaves, and the moss, and the ferns, and the coolness that swings through the branches, and the small tangles of vines that crawl along the soft dirt, and the creeks and ponds, and all the pools of misplaced water. The Other loves all of that, and I love all of that. So how is it that I've come to where I now find myself? As fascinating as the Other may be, I know full well that I only came to watch because it's the first step of every hunt. Such a terrible thing I must do. Because even as I find myself drawn to the Other and its curious ways, I'll do whatever it takes to keep my littles alive. That much is certain.

"Hey, honey, smells great." He took off his cap and hung it on one of the many pegs covering one wall of the mud room. "What is it?" he asked as he walked through the living room to the kitchen.

"African stew," she said, then, "Oh, can you feed Scruffy? Dinner's almost ready."

"Sure." He looked around the living room, then took a quick peek into their bedroom. "Where is he, anyway?"

Now Lydia turned from the stove and met her husband's simple question with a surprisingly serious expression. "You mean, he's not with you?"

"No. I figured he finally decided you were his preferred provider for today and followed you home."

Lydia turned the burner down low and joined Jonathan in the search for their dog. "Yeah, he did come back to me, but then, just as I was crossing the creek and nearly home, he turned around and went running back in the other direction. You know how he runs back and forth whenever we're separated."

"And I did see him again. He hung out with me for a while as I worked on a section of the trail. But then…"

"What? Where did he go?" Lydia's voice has gained a frantic edge as they both investigated every nook and cranny that might hide a small dog. They were now calling to each other from different rooms.

"I don't know. At some point, I looked down, and he was gone. I just assumed he'd made one last run back to you. Are you in our bedroom?"

"Yeah."

"Check behind my bedside table. That's kind of a favorite spot of his."

But he wasn't behind his bedside table, or her bedside table, or anywhere else their twenty-minute search of the house took them. They had no choice but to conclude that Scruffy was still out in the woods. So they put on their coats and head-mounted flashlights they kept hanging in the mud room through the winter, and headed back up the trail.

As they hiked, Jonathan tried to reassure his wife. "He knows these woods and these trails. There's no way he could have gotten lost. I mean, how many times did he bounce between us just now? He probably just found something rotten to roll around in and is taking his time wandering home."

"I don't know, Jon. I'm worried. What's the number one rule about Scruffy whenever we think he's disappeared?"

No answer was needed. They both knew full well that Scruffy was not a loner. He spent ninety-nine percent of his day within twenty feet of one of them. The one percent was made up of situations like today when the two of them split up and he felt the need to run back and forth between them. Some ancient herding instinct, they supposed.

They hiked together through the damp air until they reached the far end of their earlier hike, then slowly backtracked, knowing that once they'd returned home there would be little else they could do. Even then, Jonathan tried to stay positive, and they clung to a reasonable hope that they'd be woken in the middle of the night by the scratching at the slider, Scruffy's preferred method of gaining entrance to the house.

But morning came, and there was still no sign of him. It was time to get others involved in the search.

Chapter 10

You see why I had to take down the dog, don't you? I mean, with
both littles starving and looking up at me like that, and there's
that thing out there yipping and yapping. It may be distantly related to the dogs that long ago roamed these woods with dignity
and respect, earning their kills like the rest of us, but this thing
was a long way fallen from that. We used to have quite a game
of dogs and cats in these woods a hundred thousand years ago,
competing for prey, although we seldom went after each other.
But that was a long time ago. Yesterday, that thing was living in
a dream world, and he went down five minutes after I made the
decision. It wasn't any contest, believe me. Got to hand it to the
little thing, though, it did everything it could to warn them about
me. It made me from way down the trail, and it kept barking and
barking, practically screaming at them that they were getting awfully close to a very big and very dangerous cat. Loyalty, I suppose. That must be why humans partnered with them. The poor
thing knew it would be the first to go, but it stayed tight with
them the whole time, doing everything it could to save them. But
the Others seem to have fallen quite a ways themselves. They
also seem to be living in a dream world, never once concerned
that their dog was suddenly going crazy on them. Maybe that's
the difference now. Maybe the Others used to have a hidden
weapon but they lost it, kind of like how the dog lost what used
to earn it respect in these woods. They're just not what they used
to be.

But I hope you can see how I really had no choice. And it was so
worth it. When I first saw it, I thought it was only a little bigger
than a rabbit, but this thing has eaten like three or four rabbits. I

gorged myself, then curled up and let my insides turn it all into milk for the littles. Soon, I'll let them have at it, and they'll feed even better than myself. It's been a very long time since we've had such life breathed into us. If I hadn't taken the dog, right now we'd all be lying around in this den just waiting to die. But now, everything's changed. The memory of new life is spreading from our bellies and filling us with hope. To be full, to remember a tomorrow. These are things we haven't felt for a very long time.

Chapter 11

David, the current president of the community LLC, sounded especially tired, but still he tried to make his voice convey the seriousness of the meeting.

"All right, we might as well get started. As I'm sure you know, this is an emergency meeting, and we don't have very many of these, so let's get right down to business. I summarized the situation in my email, but I think it would be a good idea if Lydia or Jonathan could tell us what this is all about."

Both began at the same time before Jonathan yielded to his wife. "Well, you already know that we, well, Jonathan really, have been working on a snowshoe trail that sort of parallels *Skunk Brook*—the brook itself, not the trail." She paused for some confirmation and after a few visual thumbs up, she continued. "Yesterday, Jon and I were up there hiking and of course we took Scruffy with us. Since I needed to start dinner, I headed back while Jon wanted to continue exploring the area. Now, I'm not sure if you've seen this before, but whenever we separate, it kind of freaks Scruffy out and he keeps running back and forth between us until he eventually chooses one of us to stay with. Yesterday, though, each of us arrived back at the house and neither had Scruffy. We just assumed he was with the other. As soon as we discovered he was missing, we retraced all of our steps in the dark, but couldn't find him. Even though he's deaf, he still would have seen our flashlights if he was anywhere near us. So we're not sure what to do and asked for this meeting mainly to get some advice. Maybe one of you has had a similar experience?"

No one jumped in right away, and the couple were beginning to doubt the somewhat radical idea of calling an emergency meeting, but they were encouraged by all the thoughtful, concerned faces stacked in a grid across their Zoom screen.

"Maybe we should call the police," was the first suggestion.

"Are you kidding? They don't even file a missing person report until someone's been gone for three days. They'll laugh you off the phone."

"So what about the SPCA?"

"I don't know. They'll probably file some paperwork and maybe come out to visit, but how are they going to help find Scruffy? Plus, I think they're required to inform the cops."

"What's everyone got against the police, anyway?" Objected Sam, the single owner of a cabin on lot five.

"Nothing. I just don't know what they could do. If Scruffy's lost, and we are assuming he's out there lost, right, then we're the best ones to go out and look for him."

Now Jonathan spoke up. "I can't believe he'd get lost since he's been back and forth on those trails so many times. Maybe he fell and broke a leg or something."

"That's possible," said David, "but then wouldn't he be right there on the trail?"

There was a protracted silence before Lydia spoke in a quiet voice. "Listen, I know it's not likely, but the trail goes right by some spooky-looking small caves that really creeped me out as we went by them. Is it possible a mountain lion could have…you know…"

"Couldn't have been a lion," came a lone voice not associated with any of the videos currently displayed. "Catamounts are extinct. The last one was killed over forty years ago, and there have been no confirmed sightings since then."

This elicited a surprising amount of chatter from the group. The loudest voice was William's. "Uhhh, I know that's the official line, but I swear I've seen catamount prints in the mud around the edge of the big meadow. Twice I saw them."

"Bullshit. Probably a big dog."

"Hey, I'm not saying I'm an expert, but I know the difference between a dog print and a cat print, and this was definitely a cat print. A big cat print."

"And I read somewhere that scat found near Waterbury had been positively identified as catamount scat."

"Probably planted. Look, we can argue all day about catamounts, but that's not going to help find Scruffy. I mean, I'm not saying some wild animal may have gotten him. We know there are bears and coyotes."

"I agree," said David. As President and moderator, he rarely gave opinions, so the few he volunteered were usually taken seriously. "Unless there are any other suggestions for what we, as a community, can do, then I suggest we organize some kind of a search. The earlier, the better."

In addition to Lydia and Jonathan, only four people were available to participate, and none of them were available until five o'clock, at which time the sun had already been blocked from the vast majority of the forest floor. Still, Sam was eager to use his new drone camera to search the hillside from above, periodically taking photos that they could all review later. The rest of them broke up into two teams and divided up the trails nearest to where Scruffy had last been seen.

"I think it's best if we don't stay out after dark," cautioned Lydia.

"I agree," said Jonathan.

"Yes, but…" started Greg, who had shown up with his partner,

Nils, but second thoughts left his words hanging in the air. "What is it, Greg?" prompted the always curious Jonathan.

"Oh, I was only going to say that there's going to be a full moon tonight, and it'll be rising early, so it may stay bright enough to see pretty well out here for a few more hours."

Jonathan thought it over, then replied, "If you and Nils feel comfortable continuing that long, that's fine with me. In fact, we'd be very grateful. But Lydia and I will be aiming to get home by seven, and we're not expecting you guys to stay out too late."

"Yeah, we don't want to have to send out another search party for you," laughed Lydia, but it was a nervous laugh. The exhaustion of hours spent worrying was beginning to show. "I'd appreciate it if everyone could be back by dark, and let's touch bases by phone later tonight."

"Sounds good," said Jonathan. He clapped his hands to set things in motion. "Let's get going, then. Oh, and remember to stop to listen very carefully from time to time. If Scruffy's hurt, then it's likely he'll be making some kind of noise, especially if he sees you close by."

With that, each team went their separate ways to the sound of a small drone that had already lifted into the twilight and was slowly floating toward the higher ridges.

Chapter 12

From Anderson's Standard Manual of Trail Building:

Drainage and Erosion

Of all the challenges facing the trailmaker, water is perhaps highest on the list. From light drizzle to prolonged downpours to quick spring thaws, water in and around the trail is inevitable, usually frequent, and very unpredictable. The goal, of course, is to minimize the erosion of both the trail and the surrounding hillsides. In fact, regardless of the challenge or the actions taken to address this problem, it is important to always consider the effect on both the trail and the ecosystem through which the trail is built.

The first rule of thumb is to route the path in a way that avoids any places where water tends to gather or flow. A good knowledge of the terrain in all seasons is critical. It's risky business to survey a plot during a stretch of good weather and presume to know where water will congregate simply by observing the dips and folds of the topography. Water runs below grade as often as it runs above grade, and it can be quite fickle in choosing those mysterious locations where it disappears or re-emerges. Similarly, what may appear to be a natural gully may remain dry even in the most torrential rainstorm. So if at all possible, don't begin construction before you've walked the area numerous times throughout the year.

Marshlands and any lowlands harboring standing water are of course to be avoided. Likewise, trails should never follow seemingly dry creek beds, although this is a common error of novices, since they can be so inviting with their sandy flats, gentle gradients, and lack of annoying trees and branches. But, in time, water will clog the trail with sticks, logs, and rocks. Worse yet, *improvements* may serve to deny the landscape a natural waterway, causing unnecessary erosion on higher slopes.

Despite even the best route planning, though, some sections will need physical intervention to minimize the inevitable erosion. For example, it's nearly always impossible to avoid routings that run along the side of slopes, and at times these slopes may be steep. In these situations, it is essential to flatten the path, since the human foot was not meant to comfortably walk while tilted more than five percent. The simplest method, which may be all that's needed for most slopes, is to make a triangular cut along the upslope side of the trail and transfer that material along the edge of the downslope side. Do NOT transfer the material onto the trail itself. This is also a common error of novices. The below illustration demonstrates the proper technique.

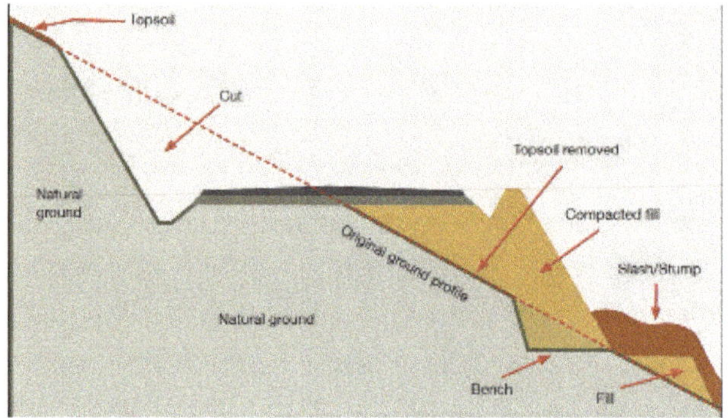

On steeper hillsides, more support will be needed, both for the trail itself as well as the upslope terrain. Usually, this is addressed by retaining walls of various sizes, depending upon the slope and the type of ground material. If the material is mostly solid rock or large boulders, little or no additional support may be needed. Generally, the finer the material, the greater the need for physical support. One thing to keep in mind is that, nearly always, if you're building a wall on one side of the trail, then you should also be building one on the other side as well. There's no point preventing debris from sliding onto your trail if debris from the trail itself is going to be sliding down the lower hillside. The only exception is a situation where only one side of the trail borders an incline and the other side borders flat terrain.

In building these kinds of support walls, large rocks or boulders are usually your best construction material. Large logs can also be used, but are subject to degradation over time. Perhaps the most important thing to remember is to assure the wall is held in place by a foundation bed well below grade; how deep you need to go will depend on the height of the wall and the steepness of the grade, but do not make the common error of just placing rocks on the ground next to your path and expecting them to do much besides providing an impressive display for those ignorant of proper trail-making techniques. Shown below are examples of both a poor construction as well as a very sturdy construction practice.

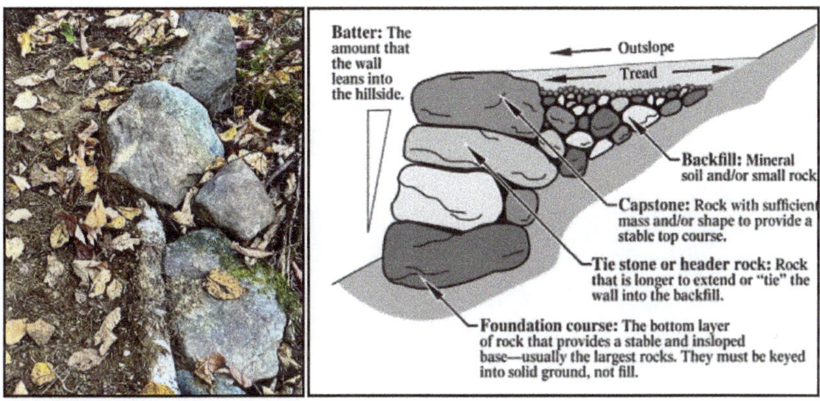

Author's Comments

What I find most interesting about Andersen's manual is that he chose not to include a chapter dedicated exclusively to route finding and determination. Instead, he addresses this topic when discussing other, construction-related, topics, and then only as it relates to this topic. For example, in this chapter, he advises against routing through a stream bed and to be wary of seasonal runoff. While I agree with this advice, I would have also added at least a few words addressing routing directly. The closest he comes is in the introduction, where he specifies that "the route of a trail should always satisfy the following requirements: a) it should be the most direct path between the starting and ending points while still satisfying b, c, and d below; b) it should assure a gentle gradient, or at least the minimum gradient possible while still meeting the abilities of its intended users; c) it should minimize unnecessary curves and switchbacks; d) it should facilitate construction and maintenance; and e) it should take advantage of whatever scenic attractions might be accessible."

While I respect Anderson's experience in trail construction and find much of the information in his guide to be quite valuable, these notes cause me to question how much time he spends out on the trail as a hiker and not as a builder. I believe trails should be made by avid hikers who are out for the fun and, yes, even the excitement of the sport. True enthusiasts aren't looking for peace and relaxation, or as some way of getting in touch with their inner selves, as if the woods were some kind of sensory deprivation tank, and they're not there because their doctor has told them it's easier on the knees than whatever sport they used to enjoy. Real hikers look ahead and feel their heart speed up as they see

the trail get skinnier and skinnier until brushing shoulders with a maple sapling becomes inevitable, and they appreciate that the trailmaker had the gumption to force such an encounter. They know a trail is not just an enjoyable and scenic way to get some exercise. It's also a track, but one that need not be raced to yield excitement. The ups and downs of a line of smooth dirt riding the waves of a minor ridgecrest can deliver all the thrills of a roller coaster ride. A trailmaker needs to understand this if he is to satisfy his true audience.

That said, my own comments are short.

Trail Routing

And let's face it, this is the only thing that really matters. Everything else is just technical. I've heard that a trailmaker should do everything possible—use every construction technique available, to make a trail appear as if it's been there for ten thousand years That, I'm told, is the sign of a great trail. I disagree. I suggest going out and finding a trail that really has been there for ten thousand years. Once found, only some minor upkeep should be needed.

Chapter 13

I've got to do everything possible to avoid what seems to be more and more inevitable. Maybe soon. Today? Tomorrow? At least when it's over, I'll know I did everything possible to keep it from happening. So I've decided to move the den higher up the mountain, to be further away from the Other and all the places where it's been spending so much time lately. If nothing else, at least it'll keep it from accidentally stumbling into the den during one of its many wanderings.

It's not an easy thing for a mother cat to move the den. It takes a lot of leaving the littles by themselves, both together and, for the first time, by themselves. There's no telling how each is going to react to being left entirely alone, and there's a very real possibility that one or both may disobey and refuse to stay put when I give the order. But that's not until later, much later. First thing is to find something suitable. They whine something fierce when I leave, but this is nothing new for them and they have no idea of what's to come, so I don't even bother to look back as I make my way slowly to the first good lookout over the canyon. Quiet, empty. Empty of the Other but empty also of any signs or sounds of prey, because I'm still holding out some hope for Plan B. Until recently, a cat could always find a deer to hunt down in this part of the forest, but the noise of those monsters busy night and day building still another den (if you can even call it a den) for the Others has pushed them onto the high slopes of Bald Hill, and that's too far away from my littles for me to venture. At this point, I'm not even sure I could catch up to one, given how hunger has weakened me. I'll still give chase, though, if I should spot one.

I leave at the darkest hour of the night, trying to avoid being seen by bears or coyotes as I slip out of the den. That gives me several hours of searching before there's even a hint of light on the horizon. The secrecy of both dens is critical to the survival of the littles during this dangerous transition. Sleeping predators are also less likely to hear the whimpers and whines of baby catamounts, so I need to be quick and stick to this timing even if I find nothing.

I head up the canyon in the exact opposite direction from which the new trail has been approaching us over the past month, creeping along the slopes of Cobble Hill while slowly gaining elevation. Even though the creek would give better access to water, it's also a likely avenue for the trail and in general is more likely to be frequented by Others. This eastern slope is littered with huge boulders and broken by many very high cliffs, so I'm hopeful of finding a good, well-hidden shelter for the three of us. There's one place in particular that I came across in my earlier search before finding our current den where I gave birth, the only place two baby cats have ever known. It's near the base of a cliff further up the canyon, where the slope levels off to form a flat area next to the creek. Even though it's high enough up the cliff so as to require a single full Catamount leap (which would isolate us from most animals), its proximity to such a level and watered area meant too much traffic, specifically bear and coyote traffic. Yes, there are others capable of making a meal of them in my absence, but my scent will keep most of them away. Around here, only bear and coyote might be brave enough to investigate. I know there's a bear with her cub who patrols these woods, as well as one very small and somewhat pathetic pack (if three even qualifies as a *pack*) of coyotes who move as if they are as starved and weakened as myself. Even though that den could be a last resort, it's not in a very sensible location, so I stay alert for any alternative as I sneak along the base of one of the highest and steepest cliffs on this side of the ridge.

Leaping up from the forest floor to a higher rock ledge should be easy for a cat of my size, but my hind paws land shy of their mark and clatter uselessly against the granite face. Fortunately, I manage to get most of my weight onto the shelf and my front paws react by reaching further forward in an attempt to latch onto something, but there's nothing but a flat ledge and, having relinquished what little purchase those paws had gained, I slowly begin to slip backward. It's a hopeless position, so I push off with my hind paws, flip my body around mid-air, and land safely back on the layer of dead leaves lining the base of the cliff. There's no point in trying again. If I can't make it on my own, I couldn't possibly do it with one of the littles in my mouth, so I continue along the base of that cliff and others nearby until I feel the pull of dawn drawing me back to the den.

But there's no need to give up entirely, and something might still come along if I return by a different route. I stay low this time, which turns out to be a bad idea; about halfway back, I find myself caught up in a steep, rocky area where the space between the rocks is overgrown with tangles of vines and beeches so young they have yet to achieve sapling status. At one point, my legs become so entwined that I desperately try to free myself with a single giant leap, only to fall forward awkwardly as the undergrowth refuses to let go of my left hind leg. Surely the Ancients looking down at me are either laughing at my predicament or growling with disgust at how low I've brought the once-proud catamount. But then I do something different, something I don't think they would have done. The only reason I say this is that, even though I'm a lonely critter these days, I've lived with lots of catamounts and I've never seen a single snagged cat do anything but struggle fiercely before taking off like crazy to get away as fast as possible. That's what my body has always done, and that's what I've always seen other cats do. But it's not what I do this time, not in this moment. Instead, I stop and gently thread each tangled paw through the clinging vines until all four are resting on the ground. Then I stop and stay perfectly still, listening for the small voice inside, the *me* that, while still distant, has recently become distinctly recognizable. Something needs attention. The tangles? As I'm trying to figure it out, I am nearly knocked over by the awful, putrid stink of nearby fox.

If only it were a fox, perhaps trapped like I am but lacking the strength to free itself. It would be like a kill delivered by the ancients. But the scent is old and it turns out to be nothing but an abandoned fox den less than a single casual leap away. Beneath the remains of a fallen beech tree smothered in vines, a

hollow has been dug out underneath a large granite slab. It reeks horribly, but is unoccupied. Not that any returning foxes would be a problem for me, even in my debilitated condition. No, they would be easy kills and a much-needed snack, but I know foxes are too smart to come anywhere near me.

The carved-out space looks to be just big enough for the three of us, and we could endure the awful smell until we replace it with our own, so I look for markers to help me find my way back to this place. Then I take a long piss on a nearby tree stump before heading back. At least I've found a decent spot.

The next night I revisit the site, setting up a good four giant leaps upslope, which fortunately also turns out to be upwind of the den. Leaving the littles by themselves on consecutive nights is a risk; animals in this forest usually keep to their set daily routines and are consequently very sensitive to the patterns of others, but I need to observe the entire surroundings of the potential new den for any signs of the coyotes or the bear with her cub.

It's a moonless night and all is quiet. So quiet, in fact, that at one point I startle myself and realize I must have drifted into a light sleep. I remember a dream, but not of tall cows this time. There were Others in this same forest, but not in ones and twos as is most often the case with occasional visitors passing through, but instead traveled in larger groups, and they all lived together out in the open where the other animals could watch and approach closely. It must have been summer in my dream because the Others wore nearly nothing at all and at times crept silently through the woods, clearly hunting deer in a way that resembled our own hunts, but I didn't see them as a threat or as competition. There was plenty of deer and other prey to provide abundant kills for all.

All of this comes back to me the moment I wake, which is very unusual; never before have I recalled a dream so vivid and detailed. Something else, too; one of the Others—a female I think—who found a broken little, one of our own catamount littles, and cared for it for nearly an entire moon before releasing it back into the woods, where we celebrated its return to the pride.

I watch and listen until I know the night is nearly over, and as I stand guard over our future den my thoughts keep returning to the Other I watched for so long the other day; the one who worked so hard tending to that tiny piece of this great wilderness. Catamounts do not cry, but they do feel, and these memories bring sadness into these brief moments unclaimed by instinct.

Photo by David Keith Jones

The following night, I fill my mouth with first one little and then the second, trotting slowly for the most part but occasionally throwing in some speed for their amusement. As we bounce between the trees on our way to the new den, each purrs and squirms lightly in my mouth, squealing with delight when I turn on the speed. It's surely the most fun they've had in their short lives.

Winter/Fall

Chapter 14

It was a lone hiker who discovered Scruffy's remains, a woman who lived two houses down the road from Jonathan and Lydia. She was one of the few locals who regularly hiked the main ski trails, always accompanied by her black Newfoundland that was so big and shaggy it was nearly always initially mistaken for a bear by other hikers. It was the Newfoundland who caught Scruffy's scent and bolted into the woods, then uncharacteristically refused to return when called, leaving his owner no choice but to follow suit. When the woman caught up to her disobedient dog, she found him sitting next to a small white skeleton. Although picked nearly clean, there were still strings of tendons and cartilage still wet with dark red blood, and flies covered both the remains and the bloody leaves and dirt surrounding the skeleton. It was clear that the animal had been killed within the past week. But was it a fox? A very small coyote?

"C'mon, Milo," she said, walking back to the trail, then grabbed the Newfoundland's collar and gave a gentle tug. It was then that she saw another collar, this one lying a few yards away, half buried in freshly dug dirt.

Out of respect for the owner, she first called the number on the tag.

"Hello, my name is Beth Winslet and I live near the end of Bert White Rd."

Lydia recognized the voice. "Yes, Beth. We've run into you several times out on the trails. You're the one with the big black dog, right?"

"Yes, that's me." She waited a moment to compose her thoughts, as the conversation had become more personal than she'd been expecting. "Listen, I'm afraid I have some terrible news. You're the owner of Scruffy, right?"

"Yes."

"Well, I'm afraid it appears as if he's been killed somehow. I'm so sorry. Maybe I'm mistaken and it's not Scruffy, but…"

"Oh God, it probably is. He's been missing for several days now, and we've been hoping he wandered off and might still show up. You say, killed?"

Beth tried to avoid any detailed description of the gruesome scene she'd stumbled upon, but Lydia's questions kept pulling it out of her. Every pause, no matter how brief, was an opportunity to end the conversation, but Lydia kept it going until she'd emptied her neighbor's mind of everything she could remember about her unfortunate discovery. When it was over, Lydia felt an emptiness that all the information she'd extracted couldn't fill.

She didn't want to face this by herself, so she waited until Jonathan got back from his shopping trip before they walked together to their neighbor's house. Lydia relayed the bare minimum of what she'd learned over the phone, and their walk was a silent, sad trudge down the hill. After so much time had passed since their dog's disappearance, they hadn't been expecting any kind of happy ending. Still, the finality was an abrupt hit, made more difficult by the shocking idea that Scruffy apparently had been attacked and killed, presumably by some other animal. As they walked, Lydia couldn't help but think of that dark cave lurking so near Jonathan's new trail, but for now she kept those thoughts to herself.

Their knocks at the neighbor's door were met with loud barks from inside, and for a moment Lydia even considered the huge Newfoundland as a possible suspect, but dismissed the possibility as she remembered how gentle it was and how well he and

Scruffy had interacted the few times they'd met.

"Please, come in. I'm so sorry about this; it must be awful for you right now," said Beth, waving them inside.

Jonathan stepped forward, but Lydia stayed put. "We were hoping to go straight to Scruffy, if you don't mind."

Beth hesitated, then answered in a quiet tone. "I think maybe it might be best to wait a while, first." This was met with understandably puzzled expressions. "It's very ugly, what happened, and for all of us living around here, well, I thought it would be good to get an understanding of what did this. I mean, you and I hike these woods nearly every day."

"I agree," said Jonathan. "But I still don't understand what we'd be waiting for."

"I made a couple of phone calls, to the police and to Animal Control, so we can get a professional analysis of the situation. They'd probably want the scene undisturbed until they get here. You know, footprints or paw prints, that sort of thing."

"The police?" Lydia tried to keep her emotions in check, but couldn't help raising her voice as she continued. "What, you think a human might have done this? Some psycho? Are you joking?"

"No, I don't think that, but I don't know what to think. That's why I wanted someone who knows better than I do to take a look. They should be here soon, and in the meantime, would you like a cup of coffee and some cookies perhaps?"

After half an hour of strained small talk and incessant glances through the far living room window to the driveway, two cars finally pulled up and parked: a cop car followed by a green truck. At least the cop car didn't have its lights flashing and siren wailing, thought Lydia as they all walked quickly to and through the front door before the visitors had a chance to knock. There were two uniformed officers—a man and a woman—as well as a third man who also wore a uniform, but his was entirely green, like something a park ranger or some other kind of nature authority would wear.

This third man kept to the back as everyone introduced themselves, as if he were there only to observe and not to participate. Finally, after they'd all shaken hands and the officers had refused Beth's offer of coffee, Lydia stepped outside the circle of pleasantries and walked over to this third man, reaching out her hand to him.

"Hi. My name is Lydia Prester, and this is my husband, Jonathan," she said, pointing to Jonathan, who had followed his wife and now stood alongside her. "We live a few houses up the road, and it was our dog, Scruffy, who was attacked. At least we think it was Scruffy, although we haven't been shown anything yet."

Her sharp look at Beth prompted a reply even before the third man could answer. "We thought it best to leave the site undisturbed, so you folks could do your work properly."

The man didn't respond to this last comment, but did accept Lydia's hand into his own in what was more of a quick and gentle hold, rather than a real handshake. "It's nice to meet you, Lydia, and you too, Jonathan," he said. "My name is Chris Wilkinson and I'm with the State Animal Control Department."

Chris Wilkinson had been way overqualified for his position when he'd joined Animal Control four years earlier. Despite having achieved both a Bachelor's Degree in Paleozoology from the University of Vermont and a Master's Degree in North American Temperate Zone Wildlife Biology from Cornell, Chris now found himself crawling under porches to retrieve sick (and sometimes dead) skunks. Occasionally, he'd get the chance to rescue abused animals from their usually mentally disturbed owners, or even participate in a complex operation to relocate a bear who'd become a campground nuisance. But most of his calls involved the removal of skunks, beehives, raccoons, and other usually harmless creatures from the vicinity of nervous homeowners. So when he was assigned a case of a pet apparently attacked by a wild animal, he raced eagerly up the hill from his office in Williston. This wasn't something you see every day, and he wanted to make the most of it. Before leaving the office, he'd gathered together everything he might possibly need, since he knew you only get one chance at a fresh crime scene: a collection kit with extra isolation bags, dissection tools, several sizes of electric surgical saws, as well as a large one in case he needed to clear any debris from the area, the station's best camera with two macro lenses, five plaster casts, along with a notebook and tape recorder to capture his thoughts and impressions as he did the field analysis.

"We've been waiting for such a long time," Lydia practically begged him. "Can we please go and see our dog Scruffy?"

"Yes, of course. If you can wait just a few minutes, though, there's some stuff I need to get out of the van and take with me to the site. I also need to ask you just a few questions. If you want, you two can tag along as I get my equipment. That may speed things up a bit."

"Of course."

Chris gestured to a small black rectangle clipped to his belt. "You mind if I click this baby on so we have a record of the conversation?" This brought out some hesitation, so he added, "It's really just to keep me from having to write everything down, that's all."

After getting two nodding heads, he called over to the cops, who were talking with Beth. "Hey, you guys have any problem with me interviewing these folks while I get my kits out? I'll share everything, and it'll give you a chance to get all your stuff ready."

In concert, both cops looked up and replied, "Yeah." But in fact, they hadn't brought any investigative tools whatsoever. After all, this was small-town Vermont and not *CSI: Los Angeles*. They were prepared to break up a fistfight if necessary, but that was about it, so as they continued to chat with Beth, Jonathan and Lydia recounted to Chris the entire story still one more time. He did interrupt a few times to confirm the date Scruffy went missing, as well as the specific times of all their activities that day, and from time to time, the three up front would look back at Beth to point them in the right direction until finally their neighbor shouted at them to stop, that this was the place.

They stood there for several minutes as Beth scanned the wooded hillside above the trail, looking for something to reassure her that this was indeed the right spot.

"I should have brought Milo," she muttered, still puzzling over uphill terrain.

"That would not have been possible," answered Chris. "The dog would only further contaminate the scene. It's OK, there's no hurry. Take your time, and if this isn't it, then we can continue up the trail."

This seemed to give the hesitant woman a burst of energy, and she jumped the drainage ditch bordering the path and marched quickly uphill. "No, this is it. Now I remember."

The first few minutes were easy walking through open, mature woodland, but soon the easy walking devolved into true bushwhacking as they dipped into a ravine clogged with low brush and tightly spaced beech saplings. The ground also became more uneven and rocky, causing everyone to slow down to eyeball each footfall.

"This is promising," Chris said to Lydia as they reached out to clear branches out of the way. "It's starting to look more like the kind of place where an animal would bring a kill."

Sure enough, just then they heard the proclamation from Beth that they had arrived. She was at the bottom of a rocky but dry creekbed. "Got it," she yelled, and the others picked up their pace, anxious for that first view.

"Wait a second. Everyone freeze. Please stay in place for a few minutes. It's important that I begin my analysis before everyone stomps right up to the site. So stay put for now while I take some photos, check for prints, and collect some preliminary evidence. Beth, if you could also back away slowly, retracing the same steps you took in, if at all possible."

It was clear that no one was happy with this instruction, but they all understood why it was needed, and there was no grumbling heard.

Chris pulled a roll of yellow tape from his jacket pocket and asked Jonathan and Lydia to tape a wide outline of the site. Then he very slowly approached the kill, careful not to step on any prints along the way. The ground was soft, and the previous visit by Beth and her dog was quite visible. In particular, the huge dog's paw prints were all over the place, which would make it more difficult to collect evidence.

The moment he looked down at it, he knew something didn't fit. In his mind, he'd been reviewing typical kill sites for the four most likely candidates: bear, bobcat, coyote, and fisher cats. The problem was, what he was looking at didn't seem to fit any of them. Coyote was the easiest to rule out, since they always hunt in packs and the kill would have been torn to bits, with bones and fur spread over a wide area. Bear had always been a remote possibility since bears do not hunt small animals. A bear might kill a pet, but only if surprised or if the pet came close to a mother's cub, but it's very unlikely the bear would feed on such a kill. Fisher cats were harder to exclude with any certainty, but even though Scruffy was a relatively small dog, she would still have been twice the size of any fisher cat around here, and Chris couldn't remember a single reported encounter between a fisher cat and any pet. Possible, yes, but very unlikely. That left bob-cats. It would have to have been a very large, very brave bobcat, and a very strong bobcat based on the number and size of the broken bones in the carcass. But bobcats are so very shy, especially of humans. Based on what he'd been told, Scruffy must have been taken while she was still fairly close to Jonathan, and it was very unlikely a bobcat would have remained anywhere near the two of them. No doubt, it was a puzzler.

There wasn't a whole lot of evidence left at the scene. Drag marks but no Scruffy prints; as suspected, the poor dog had been killed elsewhere and brought to this location for feeding. No human prints other than Beth's, but there were several large animal prints that appeared to have come from a cat—support for the large bobcat theory. He took pictures of everything as well as casts of the unidentified prints, bagged up the entire carcass, and readied himself for the trip back down to Williston. It had been a good day, and he began to think about giving this job a little more time. Maybe today hadn't exactly been CSI: Honolulu, but it had been a step above chasing skunks through crawlspaces.

Since Jonathan and Lydia wanted to spend some additional time together at the site, Chris and the others said their goodbyes there and pushed homeward through the tangled forest.

Chapter 15

When he returned to his office, Chris cleared the surface of
his desk and carefully laid out all the evidence he'd collected.
Mostly photographs, but a few casts and specimen jars of blood-
stained soil and leaves. The carcass had already been shelved in
a small freezer near the station entrance, and he knew that before
long the casts needed to go into the bake-oven, but he couldn't
help examining them once more, this time with the aid of a bright
light and a magnifying glass. It was clear to him the prints had to
have come from some kind of cat, and the fact that they accompanied the drag marks strongly suggested that they belonged to
Scruffy's attacker. In his mind, he corrected himself; not *attacker*
but *predator*. From the way the carcass had been picked clean of
all edible tissue, Chris had no doubt the dog had been killed for
food by a predator desperate enough to target a pet in the vicinity
of its human owner.

He slid open his top drawer and took out his steel rule, then laid
it next to one of the casts. A bit over seven centimeters would
make it one hell of a large bobcat, that was for sure. But what
other cats were there in Northern Vermont? Maybe a stray lynx
that wandered down from Quebec? He bent over to get as close
as possible and took a picture with his cellphone, then entered it
into an animal print identification app he used from time to time.
The app returned only one result: mountain lion. Quite definitive,
except for the fact that there were no mountain lions in Vermont.

After walking the casts to the oven, he took the long way back
to his desk to confirm there was no one else around to provide a
fresh set of eyes on this whole situation, but no such luck. So he
dug out his notebook from his coat pocket and punched a famil-

iar number into his cellphone.

"St. Johnsbury Animal Rescue, how can I help you?"

"Hi Elaine. This is Chris from over in Williston."

"Chris, how're you doing? Hope things are quieter on your side of the state."

"Well, kind of. It actually hasn't been very busy here, but I do have a mystery on my hands."

"Ooh, a mystery. I love mysteries. Please, do tell."

"OK, but it might take a few minutes. You got the time?"

"Of course. Fire away."

Chris gave his associate a condensed version of the day's events, grateful that it was Elaine who'd picked up. She had more experience than anyone else he'd worked with, and in fact, he'd spent most of his training time tagging along behind her. If anyone could figure this out, it'd be Elaine. Still, there was too much silence between them after he finished his story.

"Hmmm, that's a tough one," she admitted.

"Yeah, but here's the thing, and it's one reason I called you guys, apart from your own expertise, of course." He paused a moment, then continued. "Because I know Eastern Mountain Lions have been known to migrate between states and even between entire geographical zones. If that's what we're looking at here, they'd have to have come from somewhere, and that probably would have been noticed. I suppose that's a long way of asking if you guys have seen any signs of mountain lion activity over the past couple of years."

Elaine laughed. "Now that's something you don't need an expert for, but I can tell you absolutely that we haven't seen anything remotely resembling a mountain lion in these parts, and that would go for the Northeast Kingdom as well, because I'm sure

I'd have heard about something as exciting as that. In fact, you guys would also have been copied on something like that."

"You're right," he said, disappointed but not surprised. "I suppose I could look to the west, then. You have any friends in the Adirondacks?"

"Yeah, except lions haven't been known to swim across large bodies of water like Lake Champlain."

Chris had seen this coming, but still had no real answer. "I don't know. There are islands, bridges, ferries…" At this he couldn't help but break out into laughter, imagining a pride of mountain lions sneaking onto a ferry. "OK, I admit it's a remote possibility, but I don't have any other explanations right now."

"I can give you two right off the bat," said Elaine. "The first is that whatever app you're using is just plain wrong and you're looking at one giant bobcat."

Now Chris interrupted. "It's not just the app. I'm looking at these pictures and I'm seeing exactly what I used to see out west in mountain lion country."

"And that brings me to the second possibility, that it's a real-life catamount come back from the dead to haunt a little pocket of the Greens. Exactly where did you find this kill again?"

"On private property, undeveloped wilderness that borders Camels Hump State Park on its eastern edge."

"Wait, hang on a second." Chris could hear the sounds of drawers opening and closing, then the loud rustling of paper. "Call me old-fashioned, but I still prefer paper maps. OK, let's see… Yeah, like I thought, Camels Hump is the largest state park by a long shot, and just a few trails pass through it. Granted, a couple of those are heavily used, but there are large sections that never get visited, except by maybe a few stray cross-country skiers who like to go backcountry. This is exactly where a near-extinct animal could avoid detection for twenty, thirty, forty years even."

Chris' face scrunched into a confused knot. "You can't be serious. You mean, you actually believe those crazy tales!"

"I didn't say I believed them, but some of them aren't so crazy, and it's not impossible for a small group of animals to hide out like that for long periods of time. Just because we haven't seen them doesn't automatically make them extinct."

"This is blasphemous," joked Chris. "I'm reporting you to the authorities."

She laughed along and replied, "Fine. I'm too old to care."

There was a long silence as both of them considered possible next steps. After a couple of minutes, Elaine made a suggestion.

"Now, this is your case, so you can do whatever you want, but I'll tell you what I'd do." Chris said nothing, waiting for her to continue. "You said you've still got the dog's carcass. I'd send that thing in for a full necropsy, including DNA analysis. That would settle it for sure."

"Jaime would never sign off on that for something like this. It's like three thousand dollars. No chance."

"Which is why I'm going to be the one to approve it. Yes, you'll fill out the form online and you'll send in the carcass, but you can use St. Johnsbury as the oversight station. That way, I can approve it. Just text me the request identification number once you're done, and, as our neighbors to the north like to say, *Voila*!"

"Jaime may not like it, but if it's under your station it'll come out of your budget, so I can't see him getting too upset." As grateful as he was for Elaine's offer, things were moving too fast for Chris' cautious temperament. "Tell you what," he said, "I still want to make a few phone calls to some folks in Canada and to the south, and if no one's spotted any signs of mountain lions on the move, then I'll submit the request, and of course I'll be glad to have you pick up the bill. It's awfully nice of you to make the offer."

"That sounds reasonable. Uh…" Elaine hesitated a moment before adding, "Just one thing. Can you have the DNA results sent directly to me, and can we talk it over before sharing them with anyone else? It's a delicate subject and I want to make sure we're careful to do the right thing."

"Sure," Chris answered quickly. It wasn't until after he clicked off that he began to wonder more seriously what Elaine had in mind with that request.

Three weeks after Chris had filled out all the proper forms and sent Scruffy's still-frozen carcass off to Maryland packed in dry ice, he was at his desk waiting for another dead skunk call when, sure enough, his cellphone chimed as if on cue. But the number displayed wasn't local; it was from St. Johnsbury and he knew exactly who it was.

"Hi Elaine. What's up?" He asked, although he was pretty sure he knew exactly why she was calling. What was still unknown were the results, and his nervous system couldn't help but give a quick shudder of anticipation.

"Oh, nothing really. Just thought I'd call to say hi, see how things are going on your side of the state. That's all."

"You can be such a bullshitter. So what did the DNA show?"

"*Puma concolor.*"

"Ah-ha. Just as I suspected. A bit of a shocker, don't you think?"

"Maybe, maybe not. It's all how you look at it. Or maybe I should say, it's all in how others will look at it, and that depends a lot on what we say and how we say it."

Chris leaned back in his chair and let out a long and very audible sigh. "We say what we found and we say it as plain as day: It's a catamount."

Elaine was quick to jump in. "But is it? I mean, catamount is just another name for a mountain lion, or a puma, or a cougar. There's no difference in the DNA. These are just different names people have given to the exact same species, the same animal. In Vermont, they used to be called catamounts, and a legend grew around that name, so much so that I bet if you asked most current Vermonters they'd tell you it's an entirely different animal than a mountain lion. But you and I know differently."

Now Chris' tone betrayed his growing anger at his former mentor's apparent willingness to hide the truth behind technicalities and assumptions. "Yes, but we live in Vermont, and in Vermont they're called catamounts, so if we've got evidence they're here then we have an obligation to let people know, using language Vermonters understand."

Elaine kept her voice soft and spoke slowly, trying to cool off their exchange. "Chris, there's a big difference between a small population that's managed to survive in hiding for all these years, and a single stray mountain lion that may have wandered in from as far away as South Dakota. If we make an announcement that a catamount has been found here, it's going to be very big news, believe me. And the truth is that we don't know that lion isn't a loner who somehow strayed into the Greens."

"Are you afraid the *big news*, as you put it, is going to embarrass some friends of yours, or maybe cast a shadow over our expertise?" Now another thought occurred to him. "Tell me, did the results specify if the cat was male or female?"

"That doesn't change anything. Listen, Chris…"

"So it *is* a female, then. That changes a whole lot, in my opinion."

"It's one cat, that's it. Now, if we get more reports, then we can arrange some kind of public announcement. Maybe even a press conference, and you can be the star if you want."

Chris scoffed at this, insulted but hoping that this disagreement wouldn't bring down their long friendship. "That's really offensive, Elaine. Is that what you think I want?"

"No. I'm sorry. I'm talking too quickly, and to tell you the truth, I'm still not sure what the best thing to do would be right now. I'm just trying to make you aware that it's more complicated than you might think. The catamount is an important part of Vermont folklore and history. For us to go out there and announce that catamounts still roam the Greens, that's going to have a big impact and…"

"You know that's not what we'd say. All we'd say is…"

"No wait," she interrupted right back at him. "Hear me out on this. What I'm really getting at is if, and that's a very big if, but if there really are more of them in those mountains, then an announcement like this is only going to jeopardize what remaining population might be out there."

"You mean…"

"Exactly. The hunters will be out in force. Can you imagine the number of people who'd do just about anything to bag themselves a real catamount, or what a stuffed catamount might go for on the black market? You know, not every Vermonter is a tree-hugging nature lover."

Chris didn't have a response, and he couldn't dispute her logic. Finally, he moved to close out the call. "I need to think some more about this," he said. "I'm not disagreeing with your intentions, but at the same time, I've always believed in being completely truthful when dealing with our customers and the public. Give me a couple of days to mull this over, will you?"

"Of course."

"And in the meantime, can you attach those results to an email so I can look them over?"

"Only if you promise not to share them with anyone else until we've decided what we want to do."

"OK. That's fair. Bye, Elaine."

"Bye, Chris."

It was an awfully cold ending, thought Chris as he tapped his pencil on his desktop and tried to sort through all the thoughts running through his head.

Ten miles away, in a forested ravine still encircled with yellow tape, lay the truth Chris was slowly giving up hope he would ever find. It would, in fact, disappear in the next rain that forecasters were saying would arrive the very next day. The truth was less than three feet parallel to the line of large prints that had been given so much attention by the investigators: another line of prints, unseen and unimagined at the time; the tiniest of paw prints laid down by an animal light enough to make impressions in the mud so shallow as to be nearly invisible to the naked eye.

Chapter 16

It's hard to think of a moment of time existing before and after
the event crest. We've grown used to thinking of it as whatever
is happening *now*, and therefore as something which didn't exist
yesterday and will no longer exist tomorrow. In this way, we
are a bit like a small child who believes his mother doesn't exist
unless she is with him, or *in his space*, so to speak. Of course,
the child comes to realize that we don't have to share space with
someone or something in order for it to continue to exist. But
even though we easily accept this for the spatial world, it's much
harder to grasp the same concept for the temporal world: that a
moment of time can continue to exist before and after we happen to share its time. It's so much harder to conceptualize, even
though objectively we know that time and space obey the same
rules of physics.

I promised earlier to shed some light on a big question which
likely has occurred to you if you are giving these wild ramblings
even the slightest gift of credence. If a moment, or period of
time, exists as a wave whose amplitude crests at the *now*, or
*event cres*t, how does it carry all of the information, feelings,
spirit, etc. that is unique to the moment itself? Certainly it can't

look like this, because then all moments would be the same:

But neither can it look like this, because, though this model ac-
counts for the uniqueness of each moment, it doesn't account for

how this uniqueness could be perceived before or after the event crest.

We are left, then, with one solution to account for both uniqueness and the ability to be experienced from a temporal distance (the way a place can be experienced from a spatial distance). The wave must look something like this:

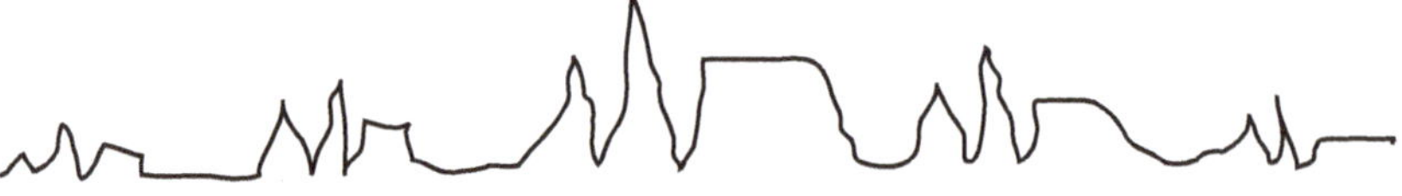

Before I abandon these last ravings, it's worth considering some of the cultural ramifications of this theory. I mentioned earlier that the perception of a *lost moment* is a rare occurrence, and even the vast majority of those rare occurrences are entirely unnoticed because they do not trigger a memory. Of those that make it this far, very few will be recorded or captured in a way that can be shared with others. It is the artist who takes this last step. Artists often say they do not create but rather merely reproduce what has been shown to them, a genuine expression but one which is often dismissed. Perhaps we shouldn't dismiss these claims so easily.

Chapter 17

Lydia had been invited to accompany a friend of hers to New York City for the entire weekend. It was an important professional exam, and the friend thought that Lydia's companionship might prevent her from suffering a full nervous breakdown just before the start of the test. So Jonathan had the house to himself for a couple of days. However, he'd been placed under some quite strict and unquestionably binding restrictions during his wife's absence.

At the LLC meeting three days earlier, during which everyone had been informed that Scruffy had been the victim of either a large bobcat or a small mountain lion that had possibly wandered down from Quebec, the community had agreed on three new requirements. These were to be temporary and would be reviewed at the next meeting. Jonathan had voted for them, mainly to be a good sport and more importantly to preserve his marriage, but even in doing so, he had no idea how these rules could be enforced. There was no discussion of observers monitoring the grounds or of penalties to be assessed for any violation. Still, he didn't disagree with any of them and had every intention of being a very good boy while Lydia was off in the big city. The rules were:

1)   Children were always to be accompanied or watched closely when outside on LLC land.

2)   Hikes were discouraged, but could be taken in groups of two or more adults. Children were not allowed on hikes. Groups undertaking such a hike must carry a canister of pepper spray, to be kept in William's garage.

3)   Bushwhacking or any venturing off established trails was prohibited.

<ol start="4">
<li>Sharing information of the attack was strongly discouraged, especially with local Vermonters or known hunters. If the attack was discussed, it would be made clear that the aggressor had been determined to be a bobcat. This one was suggested by the Animal Control authority himself.</li>
</ol>

Of course, before leaving, Lydia elicited a direct vow from Jonathan to obey these new rules in her absence. So there was no chance of Jonathan making any progress whatsoever on the snowshoe trail, despite the fact that snow could start falling at any time, effectively ending all trail construction until spring.

Except…the meadow wasn't even in the forest, so there was some question, at least in Jonathan's mind, as to whether the new rules would really prohibit a simple walk around the perimeter of the meadow. It's not like everyone was confined to quarters or anything. The intent was only to keep members of the community, especially children, away from any dangerous animal that might be out there, and since Jonathan was pretty sure of the location of this animal's den (he trusted Lydia's instincts), he could get some work done while staying far away from danger. All it took was a small change of plan. Instead of continuing to add to the existing section, he could go all the way to the other end of the trail and work backward from there. His planned end point was higher up the ridge on Stagecoach Road, so that's where he'd start, even if it meant a forty-five-minute hike along the ski trails to get there. OK, maybe he wouldn't be meeting the exact language of the new rules, but he would be meeting their intent, and wasn't that the most important thing?

It seemed to be the perfect plan, but his promise to Lydia weighed heavily on his mind as he considered it. On the third lap around the meadow, he was able to finally convince himself that she would understand his reasoning. If the pepper spray had arrived, he would have taken a can just as a precaution, but he had to laugh inside at the prospect of guarding himself against a bobcat that had managed to take down a very small dog. So he stopped by the house to grab a few tools (which could also serve as weapons) and began the long hike up Dead River Trail to its intersection with Stagecoach Road. And as he flew eagerly up the dirt road, his spirits lifted by the chill air and a low early December sun blinking at him through a kaleidoscope of recently bared branches, a catamount and her two small cubs slept, huddled together in their new home.

Chapter 18

I'm the first to hear its approach; the littles' hearing must still
be developing because they continue to sleep as it grows louder
in my ears. Even though I do my best to hide it from them, my
body's sudden switch to full alert mode is soon picked up by
my babies. Lately they've been waking straight into whimpers.
In some ways, we're all hungrier now than we were before the
kill. Yes it was glorious, and at the time it restored hope that
there might be some kind of future for our pathetic little pride (I
suppose we are as much a pride as those foxes are a pack). But
that was six days ago, the last two of which have been terrible.
Hunger has its phases. Before the kill, the weeks of cravings
and awful cramps had finally transitioned to a detached sort of
stupor. Even though it meant the approach of death itself, it had
been a relief from the active agony of the earlier phase. The taste
of fresh meat had reminded our bodies of what it was missing,
bringing back the pain that accompanies the smallest hope.

Little One soon notices my heightened awareness and restless-
ness, and he immediately wakes his sister. Before long, both
are running back and forth with all the excitement their deplet-
ed cores will allow. When I show no response to all this new
activity, they stop to catch their breaths. Little One then does
something very odd, something I've never seen either of them do
before. He clamps his tiny teeth onto the fur above my right front
paw and begins to back up in the direction of the den's entrance.
Little Two promptly joins in, grabbing another spot of fur and
pulling back resolutely. Both make small growling noises to
accompany this new exercise. I realize now what this is all about.
They're trying to pull me out of the den.

They're right, of course. My lengthy disappearance before the
last kill wasn't unnoticed, and its memory drives their feeble
tugs. We all know that if there's anything at all out there, I need

to go out and get it. Despite their tender age, hunger has over-come the fear of being left alone, and I can't ignore it. The day of confrontation I've dreaded for so long has finally arrived.

But it makes no sense for the Other to be anywhere near here; this area is far away from its usual territory. That was the whole reason I moved the den, but now its familiar sounds are getting closer and closer, as if it's stalking us. If so, then I badly mis-judged the situation and no longer have any choice but to go out and meet the inevitable head-on. With much effort, I lift myself on stiff bones, stretch out my front paws, and take three small steps toward the sliver of daylight peeking into the far side of this cramped den, swapping aside the littles with a single pawstroke. The growling stops, and there is only silence as I duck my head and squeeze through the small opening.

As always, I first take a quick look around for any obvious predator, to make sure my emergence hasn't been spotted and therefore the den's location remains uncompromised. Next, I take three giant leaps to quickly get as far away as possible—again, to safeguard the den's location. After another quick scan, I begin to slowly crawl along the side of the canyon toward the spot where the Other's little scuffling noises seem to have settled. I need to gain elevation, so getting higher up this steep wall is critical, for both viewing and hunting, so I creep up a steep, rocky creekbed, stopping at times to see if the Other has emerged into my vision.

Once atop a large boulder guarding the head of this dry ravine, I turn and look down into a clearing full of angled, uprooted stumps lying in a jumble of tangled branches. It's while I'm try-ing to make sense of this array of different shapes and lines that I become aware that one of those shapes is the Other and I am star-ing right at it. What's more, I am looking directly into its eyes.

Catamounts don't do this. I have never locked eyes with anoth-er animal nor have I ever witnessed such an occurrence. Every instinct hardwired into our bones will prevent any eye contact longer than an accidental glance, and even that will always trig-ger some kind of action: an immediate chase or a slow move to a new position. Not a flee. A catamount doesn't flee. We'll never submit to being chased by another animal, not even a bear. It's just not what we're made of. But if we know we've been spotted (and clearly even the shortest eye contact will tell you that), then we'll reposition to the start of a new hunt unless we're already close enough and all systems are go.

Which leaves the question of how this could even happen? How is it possible to maintain such an extended period of direct eye-contact? Maybe because it begins before I even realize it. The Other is blended in so well that by the time I recognize what I'm looking at, the window for my instinct to react has passed, which leaves it to the *me*. The juvenile, newly emerging, and very confused *me* that may sometimes think but is almost never called on to act. That's the body's job, and it's usually very reliable, except not this time. An accident of circumstances leaves the *me* in charge, and it freezes with hesitation. The snarl never materializes; both options—attack or leap to cover—are held in check by those eyes boring into the deepest part of the *me* for way too long, until I finally manage a weak snarl and a slow sulk back into the cover of the forest.

I hide in the woods for a very long time as the Other returns to tending its small section of dirt. It feels like defeat, like a failed hunt. My body has let me down and can no longer be trusted. But at the same time, as late and weak as my action must have appeared, it was the *me* that eventually did do what was needed, and if it can do that, what's to keep it from defying the body outright? The sun is very low now, throwing colors never before imagined through the bare December branches, and now the Other begins to follow it home. Maybe it's not so inevitable, after all.

Maybe it doesn't have to be, as I creep along the ridge top overlooking his usual trail back. It's the perfect route to stay both invisible and close enough to easily overtake it. My senses sharpen and my nose is on fire, flaring with all the hunting skill of a true-bred catamount. It's been too long since I've felt that electric current running through me.

Maybe it doesn't have to be, as I leap from trunk to trunk through the deepest stretch of forest, hearing the cries of both littles, who someday could grow to be true catamounts themselves, with all the pride and mastery of the ancients, carrying with them the essence of what it means to be a catamount.

Maybe it still doesn't have to be; maybe the *me* can prevent it, as I mount the final upslope of the next ridge over, which is the perfect place to take it down: the stand of sugar maples filling that broad space at the very top. It'll be over in seconds and I'll have my teeth in its neck, its blood in my mouth.

Maybe it doesn't have to be, but it will be anyway, and it will be the *me* to do it. From the sky falls the full weight of my newfound self-awareness, and now I know the pain carried by the Other through each and every day.

Chapter 19

On a ridge top high on the western slope of the Green Mountains in Northern Vermont, a lone catamount stepped silently through a stand of tall maples that have withstood forty years of savage winds. She was closing in on her prey, an older man who was walking briskly along a wide ski trail cut into the side of the steep ridge only a hundred feet below the summit. The trail descended slowly on its way to cross Skunk Brook half a mile further on. The catamount, however, continued to climb to the very crest of the ridge. She wanted to remain high, since remaining invisible to the prey was more important than closing the distance. She knew her speed could overtake the man in just a handful of seconds, even from her current position. The final sprint was very close now.

But just as she reached the take-off point she'd identified a few minutes earlier, she stopped abruptly at a new sound coming from a spot ahead and to the right of her. At first, it was no more than an unusual scuffling of leaves, but it was enough to freeze her in her tracks. Then, into the long seconds of her self-imposed stillness, came the unmistakable sound of coyotes. Whiny, breathy, unlike any other sound the forest could produce. Unable to immediately find a reaction to this surprising development, she stayed frozen in place, trying to quiet her breathing.

What were they doing here, anyway? No coyote would ever come within a mile of a catamount; of that she was absolutely certain. Then it hit her: *I'm downwind.* It was completely unplanned, obviously, because until that moment she'd been unaware of their proximity, but if she *had* known, she couldn't have possibly set it up it any better. Out of sight and fully downwind of a good, steady breeze. The coyotes had no idea she was even there! It was a stroke of incredible good fortune, or would have been if she'd been hunting them. But she wasn't, was she? Catamounts don't hunt coyotes, as a rule, but none of the regular rules made sense anymore. She was after the man, who was also unaware of the danger he was in, but that was to be expected. Humans were nearly always oblivious, and this man had been chosen, in part, for that very reason.

The catamount held her position and watched the three coyotes. They were clearly in stealth mode and, like her, they were also closing in on the man. Had they seen her earlier tracking him, and thus taken their cue from her? Sometimes the excitement of an imminent kill will sweep through the forest, animals picking up signals of what is about to go down, the way they pick up signals of an earthquake before the ground starts to shake. The closer you get to the event, the more signals get picked up, and in this case it so happened that the leader of the motley pack of coyotes had indeed sensed that a kill was fast approaching. Since the man was the only possible nearby prey, the pack began to stalk him and was now, like the catamount, on final approach.

The catamount, which only moments before had been finely tuned and laser focused, was now confused by this unexpected development. Her body hesitated when presented with two options. A choice of prey—one a fat, meaty morsel she could easily take in ten seconds with little risk of injury, the other a few scrawny walking skeletons who would fight her to the end, an end that would likely yield only one of them, maybe two if she were able to finish the first and inflict enough damage upon a second to make a quick and nearby death inescapable.

It happened very quickly, and without thought. There was no decision at all, no *me*. Just pure muscle memory imprinted from a time before her birth. This is exactly what the *me* had feared. But the *me* was not as smart as it thought itself to be. It seldom is.

She had no way to comprehend it, of course, but it turned out that the body, the instinct, muscle memory, call it what you will, this *automatic* part of her that the emerging but still infantile *me* had so mistrusted, deserved much more respect. Since its emergence, the *me* had always looked down on the part of her that still controlled most of her actions, considering it to be a crude and entirely selfish function with the sole objective of keeping her alive. There was good reason to believe this, since this was one of its primary responsibilities and the only one she'd thus far been made aware of. What she didn't know was that it was also capable of so much more. Buried in the autonomic nervous system given her at birth were the seeds of something much more advanced and complex than she could ever have imagined. Yes, it had been watching over her survival, doing its best to keep her own body alive, but it had also been watching over *Puma concolor*, and if ever forced to choose between the two, *Puma concolor* would win out every time. There was even a third and higher priority it was assigned to protect, but we'll not get into that now. Ideally, and most often, the interests of all three would be the same. But not always.

She flew down the slope in giant leaps, and it wasn't until the third leap that the coyotes finally spotted her, at which point they immediately abandoned their focus on the man and shifted their trajectory straight downhill at full speed. But they had pretty good instincts as well, and knew that they'd never outrun a catamount, so when they reached a level shelf, the lead stopped and turned to face the giant cat charging down at them. All three stopped and waited. Their best weapon has always been numbers. Even with a pack as small as three, it was still a pack, and there were things a pack could do that a solitary animal couldn't. So they spread out and held their ground. Two of them were able to find cover in some low bushes, leaving the third and lead coyote exposed to the ferocity of a lion in full charge.

With all the momentum built from five consecutive downhill leaps, the cat smothered the lead coyote and dug her teeth into the soft flesh of its neck, feeling the trachea snap, and then she knew it was a kill. Less than a minute to hold on and the prey would be hers. But in a matter of seconds, she heard the yapping of the other two emerging from the bush and felt the sharp pain of deep bites to her flank, in two serious wounds. There

was no choice but to let go of the first and swipe at the other
two with both paws, sending both coyotes flying through the
air. One smacked into the trunk of a dead beech tree and fell to
the ground, dazed, but the other landed cleanly enough to make
another charge. Meanwhile, the one she'd had by the throat dug
into her soft underside with shallow but repetitive bites. The
catamount tried to shake it off, but was more concerned with the
remaining coyote who was now circling behind her. She turned
to meet the threat head-on, but it was too late to prevent a strike
that delivered two deep puncture wounds to the top of her right
hind leg. Writhing in agony, the catamount finished her turn
and watched as her assailant inexplicably hadn't run for safety
following its successful attack. It seemed the coyote's teeth had
entered her from an angle that had left them buried underneath
a band of ligaments that obstructed a clean exit, and now the
coyote was struggling fiercely to extricate his mouth from the
flesh of its victim, leaving the catamount just enough time to lean
forward and crush the coyote's skull between its powerful jaws.
It was a good kill, but had come at a cost, since ripping off the

dead coyote only worsened the damage that had already been done. Blood quickly matted the surrounding fur. Too quickly, she could see, and it was then the cat knew she couldn't survive such a wound. A long, anguished cry rose from the forest floor and filled the night sky.

From the other side of the ridge, the man heard everything. Considering that he was unarmed, it likely wasn't the wisest thing to do, but he couldn't stop himself from running at full speed up the steep slope. By the time he reached the top, it was all over; all that remained was the wail of a dying catamount like a siren announcing the battle's end. He somehow knew exactly the source of that wail, and a wave of anguish welled up from within as he fell, panting, into the leaves and wind-torn branches at his feet. There he lay, unwilling to move as he listened to the muted death throes of the cat he'd known for many months. You see, he hadn't been as oblivious as the cat had suspected. He'd been following from the corners of his eyes. He'd felt her presence even when she was invisible, had smiled to himself those times he knew she was watching him work away on the trail, always asking himself what it was that kept her close, what it was that brought them so near to each other in this forgotten stretch of wilderness hidden away in the folds of the Green Mountains.

For many hours, he couldn't bring himself to rise into a blackness filled with the whimpers of pain he knew were stifled as much as possible. Because a catamount has her pride. Even as the stars rose and set, still the man and the cat didn't move.

Far away, two young catamounts also heard the wail, but only one found the courage to leave the safety of the den. Alone, she climbed boulders three times her height, pulled herself through hollows of thick mud, forged a rushing creek that swept her paws out from beneath her, until she was very close to the giver of life. There she stopped, some four leaps away and hidden in a low spot at the bottom of a small cliff, unable to face the certainty of her instincts. Unmoving, she waited, as did her mother, as did the man, the three bound together in the secrecy of their grief.

It wasn't until the sky to the west had shed its stars that the cub knew it was time to leave, time to go out and do what catamounts have always done. Tiny paws reached out over an endless wet mat of dead leaves and pulled the last catamount forward into the trees, headed upslope. Always upslope.

In the morning, the man fetched a shovel and returned to bury the cat. It was the only thing left to give her. Besides, most Vermonters had already gotten used to not having to chase after ghosts all the time. It was almost as if, at that critical moment up on the ridge when raw instinct took over, some microscopic piece of that disdained faculty had it figured out all along.

www.ingramcontent.com/pod-product-compliance
Lightning Source LLC
Chambersburg PA
CBHW041338120726
48005CB00014B/2302